LITTLE,
BROWN

LARGE
PRINT

THE SILVER ARROW

Lev Grossman

ILLUSTRATED BY Tracy Nishimura Bishop

LITTLE, BROWN AND COMPANY

LARGE PRINT EDITION

Copyright © 2020 by Cozy Horse Limited
Interior illustrations by Tracy Nishimura Bishop

Cover art by Brandon Dorman. Cover design by Sasha Illingworth. Cover copyright © 2020 by Hachette Book Group, Inc.

Little, Brown and Company
Hachette Book Group
1290 Avenue of the Americas, New York, NY 10104
Visit us at LBYR.com

First Edition: September 2020

Little, Brown and Company is a division of Hachette Book Group, Inc. The Little, Brown name and logo are trademarks of Hachette Book Group, Inc.

The publisher is not responsible for websites (or their content) that are not owned by the publisher.

Library of Congress Cataloging-in-Publication Data
Names: Grossman, Lev, author.
Title: The Silver Arrow / Lev Grossman.
  Description: First edition. | New York : Little, Brown and Company, 2020. | Audience: Ages 8–12. | Summary: Kate's humdrum life is transformed when her eccentric uncle Herbert brings her a colossal locomotive train, the Silver Arrow, as her eleventh birthday gift, leading her and her younger brother on a mysterious quest.
  Identifiers: LCCN 2020018373 (print) | LCCN 2020018374 (ebook) | ISBN 9780316539531 (hardcover) | ISBN 9780316541701 | ISBN 9780316539524 (ebook) | ISBN 9780316539517 (ebook other)
  Subjects: CYAC: Locomotives—Fiction. | Railroad trains—Fiction. | Adventure and adventurers—Fiction. | Brothers and sisters—Fiction. | Uncles—Fiction. | Magic—Fiction. | Animals—Fiction.
  Classification: LCC PZ7.1.G785 Sil 2020 (print) | LCC PZ7.1.G785 (ebook) | DDC [Fic]—dc23
LC record available at https://lccn.loc.gov/2020018373

ISBNs: 978-0-316-53953-1 (hardcover), 978-0-316-53952-4 (ebook), 978-0-316-70333-8 (int'l), 978-0-316-54170-1 (large print), 978-0-7595-5406-1 (Barnes & Noble Black Friday)

Printed in the United States of America

LSC-C

10 9 8 7 6 5 4 3 2 1

FOR LILY, HALLY AND BAZ

THE
SILVER
ARROW

Uncle Herbert
Is a Bad Person

KATE KNEW ONLY TWO THINGS ABOUT HER uncle Herbert: He was very rich and totally irresponsible.

That was it. You'd think there would've been more—he was her uncle after all—but the thing was, she'd never actually met Uncle Herbert. She'd never even seen a picture of him. He was her mother's brother, and her mother and Uncle Herbert didn't get along.

Which was weird when you thought about it. I mean, Kate had a younger brother, Tom, and he was gross and horrible, but she couldn't imagine not actually, you know, seeing him once in a while. But apparently with grown-ups that was a thing.

Uncle Herbert never came to visit. He never called. Where did he live? What did he do all day? Kate imagined him doing weird rich-people things, like traveling to remote islands, and collecting rare exotic pets and, I don't know, buying an entire gingerbread house and eating it all by himself. That's what she would've done.

But it was all a big mystery. The only thing Kate's parents were clear on was that Uncle Herbert was lazy and that he had too much money and no sense of responsibility. It made Kate wonder how such a lazy, irresponsible person could've gotten his hands on all that money, but adults never explained contradictions like that. They only ever changed the subject.

Which isn't to say that Kate's parents were bad parents. They really weren't. Parenting just never seemed to be right at the top of their list of priorities. They went to work early and came home late, and even when they were home they were always staring at their phones and their computers and making serious worky faces. Unlike Uncle Herbert, they worked all the time and were extremely responsible, though they never seemed to have much money to show for it.

Maybe that's why he annoyed them so much. Either way, they never seemed to have much time for Kate.

Kate had plenty of time for Kate, though. Sometimes it seemed like too much. She rode her bike, and played video games, and did her homework, and played with her friends, and once in a while she even played with Tom. She

wasn't one of the kids in her class who had a special talent—like drawing, or juggling four beanbags at once, or identifying rare mushrooms and telling the difference between the ones you could eat and the ones that would kill you—though she often wished she was. She read a lot; she had to be told, with tiresome frequency, to close her book during dinner. Her parents sent her to piano lessons and tennis lessons. (They sent Tom to cello lessons and hapkido lessons.)

But some days, as she pounded away at the mahogany upright in the living room or punished the garage door with her forehands and backhands, Kate found herself feeling restless. Impatient. What was the point? She was young enough that all she had to do was kid things, but she was also getting old enough that she wanted to do more than play games and pretend. She felt ready for something more exciting. More real. Something that actually mattered.

But there wasn't anything. Just toys and games and tennis and piano. Life always seemed so interesting in books, but then when you had to actually live it nothing all that interesting ever seemed to happen. And unlike in books, you couldn't skip ahead past the boring parts.

That's probably why, on the night before her eleventh birthday, Kate sat down and wrote her uncle Herbert a letter. It went like this:

> *Dear Uncle Herbert—*
> *You've never met me but I'm your niece Kate, and since it is my birthday tomorrow and you are super rich do you think you could please send me a present?*
>
> *Warmly,*
> *Kate*

Reading it over, she wasn't sure it was the greatest letter anybody had ever written, and she wasn't 100 percent sure that the word *please* was in the right place. But she thought it contained her personal truth, which her language arts teacher always said was the important thing. So she put it in the mailbox. Probably nobody would ever read it anyway because she hadn't put an address on the envelope, because she didn't know where Uncle Herbert lived. She didn't even have a stamp for it.

Which made it all the more surprising when a present from Uncle Herbert arrived the very next morning. It was a train.

Kate didn't especially want a train. It's not like she was into trains, that was more of a Tom thing. Kate was more about books, and LEGOs, and Vanimals, these cute little animals that drove vans, which everybody in her class was insane about and which she liked, too, for some reason that she couldn't really explain.

But after all she hadn't asked for anything specific, and she guessed that her uncle probably didn't have much experience with kids. So. Kate tried to be philosophical about these things.

What was really surprising, though, was

how big it was. I mean this thing was really big. Like too big to send through the mail. It arrived at their house on a specially reinforced double-wide flatbed truck with twenty-eight wheels. Tom counted. It was giant and black and incredibly complicated. In fact it didn't look like a toy at all, it looked like an actual, real, life-sized steam train.

That, Uncle Herbert explained, was because it was one.

Uncle Herbert had come to deliver it personally, in a banana-yellow Tesla so insanely sleek and tricked-out it looked like one of Tom's Hot Wheels. He was fat, with thinning brown hair and a round, mild-mannered face. He looked like a history teacher, or somebody who might take tickets at an amusement park. He wore shiny blue leather shoes and a banana-yellow suit that perfectly matched his car.

Kate and Tom came running out to stare at the train. Kate had lots of straight brown hair cut to the length of her chin and a sharp little nose that gave her a slightly princessy look, though she wasn't really especially princessy. Tom's hair

was short and blond and tufty, like a guinea pig
that just woke up, but he had that same nose,
which on him looked princely instead.

She was so surprised she couldn't think of
anything to say.

"That is a really big train" was all she came
up with. It would have to do.

"It's not a whole train," Uncle Herbert said
modestly. "Just the engine. And a tender—
that's the coal car right behind it."

"How much does it weigh?" Tom asked.

"One hundred tons," Uncle Herbert said
crisply.

"What, exactly?" Kate said. "Like, it literally weighs exactly one hundred tons?"

"Well, no," Uncle Herbert said. "It weighs a hundred and two tons. A hundred and two point three six. You're right to be suspicious of overly round numbers."

"I thought so," said Kate, who was.

You really don't appreciate how incredibly colossal a steam locomotive is till one shows up parked on the street in front of your house. This one was about fifteen feet high and fifty feet long, and it had a headlight and a smokestack and a bell and a whole lot of pipes and pistons and rods and valve handles on it. The wheels alone were twice her height.

Kate's father came out of the house too. In fact most of the people on their street came out to look at the train. He put his hands on his hips.

"Herbert," he said. "What the blazes is this?"

He didn't really say *blazes*, but you can't put the word he did say in a book for children.

"It's a train," Uncle Herbert said. "A steam train."

"I can see that, but what's it doing here? On a truck? So very close to my house?"

"It's a present for Kate. And Tom, I guess, if she wants to share." He turned to Kate and Tom. *"Sharing is important."*

Uncle Herbert definitely didn't have much experience with kids.

"Well, it's a nice gesture," Kate's father said, rubbing his chin. "But couldn't you have just sent her a toy?"

"It is a toy!"

"Well, no, Herbert, that's not a toy. That's a *real train*."

"I suppose," Uncle Herbert said. "But technically if she's going to play with it, then sort of by definition it's also a toy. If you think about it."

Kate's father stopped and thought about it, which was a tactical error. What he probably should have done, Kate thought, was lose his temper and call the police.

Her mother didn't have this problem. She came tearing out of the house yelling.

"Herbert, you blazing blockhead, what the blaze do you think you're doing? Get this thing out of here! Kids, get off the train!"

She said that last part because while all this was going on Kate and Tom had gotten up onto the flatbed truck and were starting to climb up the sides of the train. They couldn't stop themselves. With all the pipes and knobs and spokes and whatnot it was like rock climbing.

They reluctantly got off it and retreated to a safe distance, but Kate still couldn't stop looking at it. It was giant and black and complicated, with lots of fiddly little bits that obviously did interesting things, and a cozy little cab that you could sit in. It looked ominous and fascinating, like a sleeping dinosaur. The longer you looked at it, the more interesting it got.

And it was real. It was almost like she'd been waiting for it without knowing it. She kind of loved it.

Stenciled along the side of the tender, in small white capital letters, were the words:

➤➤➤ THE SILVER ARROW ➤

That was its name. They'd written it with a long, thin arrow sticking through the letters.

Uncle Herbert Shows No Improvement

"IT'S NOT EVEN SILVER," KATE'S FATHER SAID. "it's black. And what would you do with a silver arrow anyway?"

"Hunt werewolves," Kate said. "Obviously."

"And where would we even put it?" said her mother.

"Oh, I figured that out," Uncle Herbert said. "We'll set it up on some tracks in the backyard."

"On some—! In the back—!" Kate's mom was so angry she couldn't even finish her sentences. "Herbert, you are such a blockhead!"

"We're not putting train tracks in our

backyard," Kate's father said. "That's where my shade garden is going to go."

"Oh, you don't have to do it yourselves," Uncle Herbert said proudly. "I've already done it! I got some workers to do it last night. I had them use muffled hammers so you wouldn't wake up."

Kate's parents stared at Uncle Herbert.

Privately Kate thought that for a guy in a banana-yellow suit he was turning out to be a pretty sharp operator. It occurred to her that this was a good practical application of something one of her heroes used to say, which is that sometimes it's better to ask forgiveness than permission.

Grace Hopper said that. She was born more than a hundred years ago, in 1906. Back then the world was way too prejudiced to allow women to be computer programmers, and computers hadn't been invented yet anyway, but in spite of all that Grace Hopper became a computer programmer and wrote the world's first software compiler. By the time she died, at the age of eighty-five, she was a rear admiral in the navy.

They named an aircraft carrier after her. Grace Hopper was something of a role model for Kate.

Two hours later all five of them—Kate, Tom, Mom, Dad, and Uncle Herbert—were in the backyard, staring at the steam engine. It stood on a length of track on the thin burnt-yellow grass with the tender behind it. Together the two cars took up most of the yard.

Even Kate's mom and dad had to admit they were pretty impressive.

"We could charge people money to sit in it," Tom said.

"No way," Kate said. "I don't want weird strangers sitting in my private train with their weird butts."

"Don't say *butts*," said her father.

"Cigarette butts," Kate said. "Ifs, ands, or buts."

"Just don't."

"How old is it?" Tom asked.

"Don't know," Uncle Herbert said.

"How fast does it go?"

"Don't know."

"Could the strongest man in the world lift it?"

"Don't—wait, no, I know the strongest man in the world, and he definitely couldn't lift it. Want to get in?"

They sure did. It was a bit of a scramble—the train was, as previously mentioned, really big, and definitely not built for kids—but Kate and Tom were expert scramblers, and there were a couple of iron steps welded to the side of it, and a bar to grab on to.

What happened next was actually a tiny bit disappointing, if Kate was being completely honest. Being inside the cab of a steam engine isn't like being in the driver's seat of a car, or a truck, or an airplane. For starters there's no windshield, because the giant barrel of the boiler is in the way, so you can't see what's in front of you. There are two little portholes on either side, but they're not much help. It's more like a little room—the engine room of a ship maybe, but a really old ship without any computers or radar or anything.

Brass and steel tubes ran everywhere like overgrown vines, sprouting valve handles and buttons and cranks and glassed-in dials and more tubes. None of them had labels. The cab smelled like old oil, like at a car mechanic's. It was definitely real, but it was also completely incomprehensible.

There were two fold-down seats. Kate and Tom folded them down and sat.

"Now I get why train drivers are always leaning out the window," Tom said. "It's the only way you can see where you're going."

"Yeah. Too bad we're not going anywhere." Kate leaned out the window.

"Hey, Uncle Herbert, it's weird in here!"

"We don't know what to do!" Tom said. "There isn't even a steering wheel!"

"You don't steer a train," Uncle Herbert said, squinting up at them. "You just go where the tracks go."

"Oh. Right."

There was no brake or gas pedal either, or not that Kate could see.

"Is there a whistle?" Kate asked.

"Yes," Uncle Herbert said. "It's a steam whistle, though. Doesn't work without steam."

"Oh."

Kate and Tom wandered around spinning wheels and pulling levers and moving anything else that moved. None of it did anything. It looked cool, but they were kind of at a loss how to play with it. They opened a kind of stove thing set into the wall. It was full of cold ashes and soot.

Tom pretended it was a tank and stood on his seat and machine-gunned an army of invisible Nazis out the window, but you could tell his heart wasn't a hundred percent in it.

Then they climbed down again. It was all a little anticlimactic.

"You know what we should do?" Kate said when they were back on the ground. "We should connect these tracks with the old ones in the woods."

There were some rusty old tracks out there, buried in leaves and sunk in the mud—she and Tom found them one day when they were out exploring.

"Those old things?" their father said. "Been a long time since a train ran on those tracks."

"All right, everybody!" Their mom clapped her hands for attention. "It's Kate's birthday today! Who remembers when my birthday is?"

"Next week," Kate said.

"That's right. One week from now. That's how long you can keep the train. Then, as your birthday present to me, Herbert, you're going to get rid of it."

"What?!" Kate said.

"But what if I already got you something else?" Uncle Herbert said in a small voice.

"Did you get me a flatbed truck hauling

away a gigantic blazing steam train?" Kate's mom put her hands on her hips. "Is that my birthday present?"

"No."

"Then whatever it is, send it back. For my birthday you're going to get this thing out of here."

"No!" Kate shouted before she even knew what she was doing. "You can't! It's mine!"

Kate Said a Lot of Other Things, Too

KATE TOLD HER PARENTS THAT SHE HATED them and that they were the meanest and worst people in the world. She said she never got anything special or good, and even when she did they always ruined it. She said they didn't love her and all they cared about was their stupid phones.

I wish I could tell you that she said these things in a calm, reasonable tone, but she didn't. She yelled them as loudly as she could.

Then she said that this was the worst birthday ever, and her mother told her to go to her room, and she said *Fine, I will*, and she slammed the door, even though at that exact same moment her mom was yelling at her *not* to slam the door. Kate stayed in her room for the rest of the afternoon.

None of the things Kate had said were strictly true, except maybe the one about it being her worst birthday ever, although when she was two she'd had a fever and spent her whole birthday throwing up, so it was a close call.

Deep in her heart Kate knew that. She knew that her problems weren't real problems, at least not compared with the kinds of problems kids had in stories. She wasn't being beaten, or starved, or forbidden to go to a royal ball, or sent into the woods by an evil stepparent to get eaten by wolves. She wasn't even an orphan! Weirdly, Kate sometimes caught herself actually *wishing* she had a problem like that—a zombie apocalypse, or an ancient curse, or an alien invasion, anything really—so that she could be a hero and survive and triumph against all the odds and save everybody.

Which of course she knew was wrong. She

just wanted to feel special. Like somebody needed her. And obviously, having a steam engine wasn't going to make her special. *Obviously.* But she'd felt special for a bit. And now her mom was going to send it back to wherever steam engines came from.

And the worst part of it all, Kate thought—as she lay on her bed, her eyes feeling sticky from crying, and stared glumly out the window, and the afternoon stretched on and on toward evening—was that she kind of saw her mom's point. Kate hated to admit it, even to herself, but even though the train was real and awesome, it was also insanely big and kind of ridiculous, and, bottom line, it didn't really do much of anything. Given the untold skrillions of dollars Uncle Herbert must've spent on it, he probably could've bought, I don't know, a mini-submarine, or a rocket, or a supercomputer.

Or a robotic exoskeleton maybe. Anything but a stupid steam engine. Maybe he could return it and they could keep the cash instead.

Someone knocked on the door—she could tell from the knock that it was Tom. She didn't answer. He went away, tried again, went away again, then finally he just came in without knocking and flopped down on the lower bunk. They had their own rooms, but they used to share, and there were still bunk beds in Kate's room.

Tom just lay there for a while, but he couldn't stay still for long. He always seemed to have more energy than he could comfortably store in his body, and he had to burn it off somehow. He started singing under his breath. Then he started drumming along with the singing. Then he kicked the bottom of Kate's bunk. Then he pretended to be shot and fell off the bed to try to make her laugh.

Kate didn't laugh.

"Go away," she said.

"At least we get to play on it for a week. It's better than nothing."

Somebody must've told Tom once that you were supposed to look on the bright side in situations like this. She wished he wouldn't. It was annoying. Nobody ever took Tom's presents away. He never got sent to his room. Or it seemed like that anyway.

More silence. He still didn't go away.

"I think it's on fire," Tom said.

"Good."

"Why are you being mean about the train?"

"Because I hate it."

"Why?"

"Because I hate everything! Including you!"

"That's not very nice."

"I'm not trying to be nice!"

Tom was looking out the window.

"Well, it's your lucky day because the train really is on fire. Seriously. Look at it."

Kate looked out the window. She frowned. There was the tiniest flicker of what looked like warm firelight in the cab of the steam engine.

"That's strange," Kate whispered.

"Do you think it's really on fire?"

"How could it be on fire? It's made of metal."

They slipped out of Kate's room together, and out the back door onto the evening lawn. The grass was cool on their bare feet. You'd think that at this point Kate and Tom would have alerted their parents that there might possibly be a flaming steam engine on their property, but they didn't. Something interesting was happening, and Kate didn't want the grown-ups to swoop in and take it away. Not yet.

"Hey, look at that," Tom said. "More tracks."

He was right: That afternoon the train had just been on a little stub of track, but now bright new silvery steel tracks curved away from it through the grass.

"I thought that was a good idea you had," said a voice from the shadows. "Connecting them with the ones in the woods."

Uncle Herbert was standing there, leaning against the train. Kate hadn't seen him.

"It wasn't a good idea, it was a stupid idea," Kate said. "Those tracks are all old and rusty, like my dad said, and they don't go anywhere, and even if they did, the train doesn't move. In case you hadn't noticed."

"I had noticed, actually," he said. "Kids aren't the only ones who notice things, you know."

"Well, it sure seems like it sometimes."

"Well, it sure seems to grown-ups like you spend all your time watching TV and playing video games instead of paying attention to real life."

Adults always said scoldy stuff like that, but Kate was surprised to hear it coming from

Uncle Herbert. She'd been starting to hope he wasn't like that—but of course he was. All grown-ups were.

"Why should I pay attention to real life?" she said. "Real life is boring!"

"How do you know it's boring if you don't pay attention to it?"

"Well, maybe real life should pay attention to me sometime!"

"Perhaps," Uncle Herbert said quietly, like he was trying to sound all mysterious, "the world is more interesting than it appears."

"Well, that would be great." Kate crossed her arms. "Because it appears really boring!"

"What about that mysterious fire in the train. Is that boring? That is why you snuck out here, isn't it?"

"Oh, right," Kate said, brought up slightly short. "I guess it is."

She took a step toward the train, then turned back and gave Uncle Herbert a look.

"This isn't over, though."

"No," Uncle Herbert agreed. "It isn't."

It Really Wasn't Over

NOW THAT KATE WAS RIGHT UP CLOSE TO THE train, she noticed something else: White steam was floating out of a pipe on top of it and swirling around its wheels.

Suddenly she felt a bit nervous.

"Go on," Uncle Herbert said. "This is it. Real life is being interesting for a change. It's paying attention to you. Isn't that what you wanted?"

Kate didn't especially like having her own words quoted back at her, so without answering she climbed up into the cab, the metal rungs

hard under her bare feet. Inside the cab was all lit up by glowing firelight. That cold, sooty box they'd found before was actually a little fireplace, and somebody had built a fire in it. She could feel the heat coming off it in the night air.

Something else, too: Before, the tender was empty, but now it was full of coal, a huge heap of it. Tom climbed up behind her.

"Cool," he said. "It's like camping. We could sleep out here."

"It's like that cabin with the woodstove," Kate said. "That time we went skiing and Dad hurt his knee on the first day and was in a bad mood the whole rest of the week. You were little."

"I remember, though." Tom perched on one of the seats. "That was when I lost Foxy."

Foxy, full name Foxy Jones, had been Tom's stuffed fox from when he was a baby. It broke Tom's little heart when he lost him—he still couldn't read *Fantastic Mr. Fox* without crying. Weird how boys had feelings, too, but pretended they didn't.

Kate could see into the house, where her father was setting the table for her birthday dinner. He looked a thousand miles away.

"I wish it were a real train," she said quietly. "I mean I wish it could really go somewhere. Like on an adventure."

"Yeah."

Just then a big lever shifted forward with a *clunk*.

Kate frowned at it.

"That was weird. Did you do that?"

"No," said Tom.

She stuck her head out the window.

"Uncle Herbert? Something just moved in here."

Uncle Herbert looked up at her.

"What do you mean, moved?"

"Like by itself."

He frowned. "Couldn't have."

But now a couple of the brass wheels were spinning, too, and some of the needles and gauges were stirring and twitching. A couple of switches flipped.

"Uncle Herbert, really! Things are moving! Like, a lot!"

It was the first time Kate had seen her uncle look unsure of himself.

"Right. You might just think about climbing down from there." He was using that cautious tone you use when you're trying to reason with a cat. "Both of you. Maybe quite quickly actually."

"Kate," Tom said. "Maybe we should."

"But what is this? Is it a game?"

"It doesn't matter!" Uncle Herbert said. "Just get out of the train!"

Tom went to the door, but Kate stayed where she was.

"You can go," she said. "It's okay. But I want to see what happens."

Tom thought about it.

"I'm going to stay too," he said finally, in his most serious, solemn voice.

Now white steam was leaking and poofing out of the train everywhere and drifting across the lawn. A knob turned and a pure, bright white light stabbed forward from the nose of the train, lighting up the grass and the trees and the side of the house next door. From somewhere below came a sharp, satisfying *crack*. Not like something breaking, more like something that had been stuck for ages finally being released.

"That was the brakes!" Uncle Herbert yelled. "Come on! Get out!"

Chuff.

The engine made a deep, hoarse sound like an ancient beast waking up from a very long sleep and snuffing the air.

"Wait—is this pretend or real?" Kate yelled.

"It's magic!" Uncle Herbert yelled over the hissing of steam. "You didn't think I got rich by working hard, did you?"

Kate very much doubted that this was true, because unlike in books, in real life magic did not in fact exist. But right now it wasn't like she had another explanation.

Chuff...
Chuff...
Chuff...

Hissing and clanking sounds came from all over the train. The whole thing, all 102.36 tons of it, started rolling forward along the tracks as smoothly as a boat across a still pond. With something that heavy, you just knew there was no stopping it once it got going.

Uncle Herbert started running alongside the train muttering *no no no no no* to himself and trying to jump onto it like they do in movies. But somehow Kate didn't feel scared. Instead she felt as happy as she ever had in her life.

Like something in her was being released, too. Like her brakes were finally coming unstuck. This was it. This was the *something* she'd been waiting for.

Uncle Herbert seemed to be finding out that jumping onto a moving train is harder than it looks in movies.

"Come on, Uncle Herbert!" she called.

"I can't! Jump down!"

"I don't think so. It's like you said: Life's being interesting."

"But this is too interesting! Like *way* too

interesting!" Uncle Herbert stopped and bent over with his hands on his knees, huffing and puffing. "You're not ready!"

"Ready for what?"

Kate felt ready for anything. Wind was whipping her hair around. She didn't know if she was doing something very smart or very stupid, but in that moment she didn't care, because the thrill of it made her heart want to burst.

This was *so* much better than Vanimals.

Chuff.

Chuff.

Chuff, chuff...

Chuff, chuff...

Uncle Herbert tried to run after them again, but he stopped almost immediately. He really wasn't in very good shape. They were leaving him behind.

"I'm sorry!" Uncle Herbert called. "This wasn't supposed to happen! You've got a big job ahead of you, a huge job, so—just do the best you can!"

They were gathering speed now, following

the tracks across the lawn as smooth as a blade over ice.

There was just one thing missing.

"How do I blow the whistle?" Kate yelled.

"Dangly thing!"

It was the last thing Uncle Herbert said before they lost sight of him.

There was a wooden handle dangling from the ceiling. Kate pulled it, and the sound blasted out into the night:

FOOOOOOOOOOOOOOOOM!!!!!!!!

The whole neighborhood could hear it. It felt like the whole world could hear it. She did it again. And then, because she was a generous person, she let Tom do it, too.

Things Get Weirder

THE TRAIN SWUNG TO THE RIGHT, FOLLOW-
ing the tracks into the woods behind their
house, which just barely saved Kate and Tom
from crashing through the fence and annihi-
lating the neighbors' house and probably the
neighbors.

Instead they started smashing their way
through the trees.

"I can't believe this!" Kate shouted. "This
is insane!"

"Whoooooo!" Tom whooped. "Whooo!"

"I mean this is really crazy!"

The train snapped branches and shoved aside whole trunks of trees, the headlight blasting out ahead of it like the fiery white breath of a dragon. Green summer leaves flew everywhere. They were going to be in so much trouble. *So much.* They were going to pay for this *forever*! But it was totally worth it.

They knew these woods like the backs of their hands. They'd lived here their whole lives, and they'd climbed and jumped off and fallen from every tree and rock a million times. But they'd

never seen the woods at night from the cab of a giant runaway steam engine. Kate braced herself for the ultimate smash, when they would hit something big or when the tracks would run out and the whole train would lurch to a halt. It was going to be such a disaster. But so worth it. She swore to remember this her whole life: the night she rode through the woods behind her house in her own real steam train.

But the big smash or lurch never came. Instead the train kept going. Birds startled. Stiff branches scraped against the windows. She and Tom laughed hysterically. How far was it going to go?

Then Tom stopped laughing.

"Wait," he said. "What happens when we get to the hill?"

It was a good question.

In the old days, when people made maps and they came to the part where they didn't know what was there, they just drew a bunch of dragons and sea monsters instead of land. On the very oldest maps they wrote *Hic sunt leones*, which is Latin for "Here be lions."

About a quarter mile into the woods behind Kate and Tom's house there was a sudden steep hill, almost a cliff, with a chain-link fence at the top, and at the bottom was a scary dark swamp with a lot of bugs and, supposedly, a giant snapping turtle so big it could bite your foot off. If an olden-days person were making a map of the woods behind Kate and Tom's house, that hill would've been where they started drawing sea monsters. Or lions.

Kate risked sticking her head out the window.

"Oh my God. We're almost there!"

"Kate," Tom said seriously, "what's actually going to happen, though? I mean really? Should we jump out?!"

"I don't know!"

She felt paralyzed. Panicked. She was the older one, she was supposed to know! For the first time it occurred to her that maybe this wasn't going to come out okay. She wondered how deep the swamp was. If the train hit that water and sank, they'd be trapped. They could drown.

But it was too late, because even as she thought it she felt the *Silver Arrow* punch through the chain-link fence as easily as a brick through a plate glass window, hesitate for a moment like a roller coaster right before a big drop, and then tilt forward as the whole massive engine began its horrifying dive down the hill.

The *clackety-clack* of the wheels went faster and faster and faster. Kate closed her eyes and felt a sick, weightless lifting in her stomach. She clenched her jaw tight and gripped the seat till her knuckles went white....

But the end didn't come. When they got to the bottom of the hill they just kept rolling smoothly along, faster now but quieter, with no more breaking branches. Slowly she unclenched her jaw and ungripped the seat. The engine chuffed happily. Cautiously Kate opened her eyes.

They should have been sinking into the

swamp by now, with the snapping turtle waiting impatiently to snap the feet off their drowned corpses, but instead they were cruising along easily through dark, still woods.

Kate knew perfectly well that there were no woods here, there was only swamp, and after that an office park, and beyond that the highway. It was impossible.

But the woods didn't seem to care about that. They just went on getting deeper and darker.

"Where are we?" Tom whispered.

"I don't know!"

"I can't believe we're in a real train!"

"I know, right?"

"I mean what is even happening right now!"

Over the next few minutes Kate and Tom had three separate versions of this conversation, different but all basically the same. They raised the possibility that they were going to Hogwarts and decided they probably weren't, though that would've been cool, too. And it was Kate's eleventh birthday.

Kate stuck her head out her side of the cab, and Tom stuck his head out his side. She wondered where they *were* going, and whether it was a good idea to go there, and whether, if they absolutely had to, they could jump out of the train without getting badly injured, and how long it would take them to walk home after that, and how exactly their parents would punish the bejeezus out of them when they got there. They were definitely putting Grace Hopper's whole permission-versus-forgiveness theory to a serious test.

But at the same time all the excitement, all the energy, all the joy she'd been waiting her whole life to feel were finally thrilling through her whole body. Anything was worth that.

The air outside was getting pretty cold, even though it was June, and Kate shivered in her T-shirt. She was grateful for the warmth of the fire. After a few minutes she saw a pale light through the trees up ahead.

It was dim and distant at first and blinked in and out among the branches, but it got stronger and stronger till at last it came fully into view. It was a train station.

Not a fancy one, just a small country train station, a long lit platform in a clearing among the trees. There were people waiting on it.

Except they weren't people, they were animals. A few deer, a wolf, several foxes, a big brown bear, some rabbits or hares—or were they the same thing?—and a stripy-faced badger. Perched along a railing at the back of the platform was an assortment of birds, large and small.

They just stood there, as still as commuters waiting for their morning train. Each one had a ticket in its mouth.

Click-*bing*!

THE *SILVER ARROW* SLOWED, PULLED SMOOTHLY into the station, puffed out a huge cloud of white steam, and stopped with a loud hiss. There was an old-fashioned train clock on the platform, the round kind with a light inside that sits on top of a lamppost. It was late, almost ten o'clock at night.

Tom came over to Kate's side to look at the animals. The animals looked back at them. They didn't run away the way wild animals usually did. They just stood there.

It was like a dream. The air was so cold

now they could see their breath in the lights of the station.

Finally Tom said:

"Hi."

Kate wasn't always grateful for Tom's presence—in fact a lot of the time she preferred his absence—but at that moment she was. She knew she tended to hesitate and over-think things. Tom didn't have that problem, he would just blurt out anything that came into his head.

A small gray fox bent down and placed its ticket carefully on the platform.

"Hi," it said.

"Hi," Kate said.

"Been a long time since a train came through here," the fox said.

"Very long," said the badger, transferring its ticket to its paws.

Kate thought of saying *Is that so?* or *How about that!* but rejected both ideas as fatally uncool.

"How long?" Tom said.

"About thirty years," the badger said. "Where have you been? You're very late."

"Wait—just—how can you be talking?!" Kate said.

"Oh, I know," the fox said. "We do talk sometimes, just not around humans. Frankly, we don't meet a lot of humans who are worth talking to. No offense."

Kate supposed that was fair.

"But you haven't been standing here waiting this whole time, have you?" she said. "Like, the whole thirty years?"

"Oh, no. Of course not. We just look in here once in a while to check. I mean, we're animals, it's not like we have jobs."

"I guess not."

"You need to get over to the rail yard to pick up some cars, and fast," a hare said. "It's almost too late."

"The rail yard," Kate said. "Okay. Thank you. We'll do that."

It sounded like good advice.

"See you soon then."

The animals all picked up their tickets and went back to waiting. With a jerk and a loud hiss, the *Silver Arrow* moved off down the track again. Tom pulled the whistle, two quick blasts:

FOOOM! FOOOM!

Kate clanged the bell for good measure. They quickly left the lights of the station behind.

"Did you see that?" Kate said.

"I totally saw that!" Tom said.

"Those animals talked! To us!"

Not only that—and that was incredible enough—but what they'd said had made Kate's ears prick up. This wasn't just a joy-ride, Kate and Tom were going somewhere specific—namely to the rail yard, wherever that was—and for a reason—namely to pick up some cars. A joyride would've been fine, obviously, but this was even better. It wasn't just fun and games. They were on a mission. They had a job to do.

The glow of the firelight was nice, and it was starting to feel cozy in the cab. The air smelled like hot engine oil: a savory, interesting smell. Everything was made of brass and leather and wood and glass and felt very old, like the kind of place that would usually be behind a velvet rope at a museum.

"I wonder who's driving this thing," Tom said. "I mean, we're not."

"Who knows?"

Suddenly there was a click and the *bing* of a bell behind them, kind of like the click-*bing* of an old-fashioned typewriter.

Kate hadn't noticed it before, but on the wall of the cab, in among the pipes and dials and levers, was a little loop of paper. It unrolled out of the innards of the train at one end and then scrolled back into them at the other. A message had just been printed on it:

I KNOW

As soon as they'd read the words the message scrolled out of sight and more paper

scrolled out with another click-*bing*. It really was like a typewriter, or a very low-tech printer. More words appeared, neatly typed:

THE FOLLOWING ARE INSTRUCTIONS FOR OPERATING THIS STEAM ENGINE

Uh-oh, Kate thought. *Here we go.*
Click-*bing*. More words.

OPERATING A STEAM ENGINE IS REALLY COMPLICATED

BUT DON'T WORRY, I'M GOING TO TEACH
YOU HOW TO DO IT

"Great." Tom rolled his eyes. "Train school."
Click-*bing*.

IT'S NOT "TRAIN SCHOOL"

THIS IS CALLED LEARNING

WHEN DONE PROPERLY IT CAN ACTUALLY
BE QUITE ENJOYABLE

THOUGH ADMITTEDLY IT'S HARDLY EVER
DONE PROPERLY

Tom folded his arms. He looked uncon-
vinced.

LOOK, LEARNING THINGS IS INCREDIBLY
HARD AND UNPLEASANT

IF IT WASN'T THEN EVERYBODY WOULD
DO IT ALL THE TIME

**AND THEN EVERYBODY WOULD KNOW
EVERYTHING**

WOULDN'T THEY

Kate shrugged. "I guess."

YOU GUESS RIGHT

WHAT YOU NEED IS A GOOD TEACHER

FORTUNATELY I AM ONE

"Right," Tom said under his breath.

I AM RIGHT

"How can you even be talking?" Kate asked, keenly aware that she'd also just asked a fox that exact same question.

I DON'T KNOW, I JUST AM

"Are you like a giant metal robot or something?"

I DON'T KNOW

I MEAN AREN'T YOU JUST A ROBOT MADE
OF FLESH AND BONES

IF YOU THINK ABOUT IT

Kate thought about it. The train did kind
of have a point.

FOR NOW YOUR ONLY JOB IS GIVING ME
MORE COAL

THE COAL IS IN THE TENDER. JUST
SHOVEL IT INTO THE FIREBOX

THE FIREBOX IS THE BOX WITH THE FIRE
IN IT

"I figured that," said Tom.

LESS TALKING, MORE SHOVELING

There were two short shovels and two pairs

of work gloves hanging on pegs in the tender. They put on the gloves and shoveled chunky pieces of black coal into the firebox. It took only a few shovelfuls before the fire started to get hot and glowing again.

Job well done. It was surprisingly satisfying.

"So," Kate said, "I guess it's a talking train."

"I guess so."

Click-*bing*.

I GUESS SO

The Rail Yard

THE TRAIN CHUFFED ALONG; KATE THOUGHT it chuffed a little faster and more vigorously now that they'd given it more coal. She'd never had a pet, because between them her parents were allergic to every single animal under the sun, but it felt like she imagined feeding a pet would feel. Except that it was a giant metal pet that you rode inside.

Snow drifted down through the trees outside, which was very odd considering that it was supposed to be summer, but not odder than anything else that was going on. The train kept talking to them. It explained how the throttle worked, and it showed them where the brakes were. Then it told them to look out the window.

Something was happening out there. The track they were on split into two tracks. Then it split again, and again, and those tracks split, too, so that in a minute one track had become dozens of tracks curving away on either side, and soon they were in a huge open clearing completely filled with darkly gleaming rails like a giant plate of steel spaghetti.

Kate and Tom carefully reduced the throttle and applied the brakes, and the *Silver Arrow* chuffed and chuffed slower and slower till it gave out a huge steamy sigh and stopped.

All around them on the tracks were parked dozens and dozens of train cars, maybe hundreds, all different colors and shapes. Some were short and stubby; others were long and lean. Some looked old and dusty and rusty, while others were shiny and new.

It was late, but Kate felt more awake than she ever had in her life.

"This must be the rail yard," Kate said. "That thing the fox was talking about."

"He reminded me of Foxy Jones," Tom said. "What do you think we should do now?"

They looked at the paper where the train posted its messages, but it was blank and silent. Outside nothing moved. Lamps cast a soft, eerie light over everything and lit up the falling snow in a great white dome. Kate suddenly felt nervous being out in the middle of nowhere like this, with no adults around.

But then someone came walking briskly toward them across the snowy tracks. It was Uncle Herbert.

Uncle Herbert! It was so good to see him! They'd only just met him today, but it felt like seeing an old friend. He was carrying a clipboard and wearing a dorky conductor's hat and a bright yellow parka to match his yellow suit.

He stopped and looked up at them.

"Kate. Tom. Good to see you. You made it this far."

"Uncle Herbert!"

"Uncle Herbert!" Tom said. "We went

through the woods and didn't crash and then we saw a station and it was full of animals and they talked and then the train talked!"

Tom said this as one long continuous word. Uncle Herbert didn't look particularly surprised at any of it.

"How did you get here ahead of us?" Kate said.

"More magic," Uncle Herbert said. "Listen, this is all a huge mistake. None of it was supposed to happen, or not yet at least. The train left much too soon. Maybe it had to, maybe it couldn't wait, I don't know, but I don't like it. We'll be lucky if we don't all end up in the Roundhouse.

"But it's too late, you can't go back, so you'll just have to go forward and do your best. You've got a schedule to keep to now."

"Wait—we do?" Kate said.

"We need to put together a train for you right away. Fortunately, no one's come through here for years, so they've got just about everything in stock. What cars do you want?"

"Cars? You mean like train cars?"

"Yes."

"You're really going to just give us a bunch of train cars."

As with overly round numbers, experience had taught Kate to be suspicious of people offering her free stuff.

"I gave you a steam engine, didn't I?"

"Um. Okay, what are the choices?"

"It doesn't work like that. This isn't a restaurant, you're not ordering off a menu. It's your train—you have to make it up."

Kate and Tom glanced at each other.

"May I suggest," Uncle Herbert said delicately, "that you begin with some passenger cars?"

He did actually sound kind of like a waiter at a fancy restaurant.

"Sure," Kate said. "Sounds good."

"Yeah," said Tom.

"Two passenger cars?"

"Great," Kate said. "Two passenger cars."

"Excellent. What else?"

What other kinds of train cars were there? Her mind went completely blank. She really was not one of those kids who was super into trains.

"A...dining car?"

"Dining car. Good." Uncle Herbert wrote it down on his clipboard.

Kate couldn't think of anything else. "Tom, you pick something."

"Uh. We could have two dining cars?"

"What's the point of that?"

"Like two different restaurants. If we got bored of one, we could go to the other."

Kate thought that was ridiculous, but Uncle Herbert wrote it down, too.

"Second...dining...car. Good. Need a kitchen car to go with it."

"Two kitchen cars!" Tom was getting into it.

"Okay. What else?"

There was a long silence.

"A sleeper car," Kate said. "That's a thing, right?"

"Sleeper car."

"I can't think of anything else."

"Yes," Uncle Herbert said, "you can."

Kate thought of something. It was silly, but she couldn't come up with anything else.

"I would like a library car," she said. "Like a car that's all full of books, with big leather chairs and things where you can go and just read."

She was a little embarrassed, but Uncle Herbert didn't turn a hair.

"Library car." He wrote it down. "What else?"

"Movie car," Tom said.

"No movie car."

"What?"

"You can watch movies at home."

"But she got a library car!"

"And I'm sure she'll let you use it."

"This is such a rip-off!"

"Fine, I'll give you your money back. Or wait, that's right, you didn't give me any money! You're getting a completely free train!"

"I want a weapons car, then. Two weapons cars. One for swords, one for guns."

"No."

"Video—"

"Nope."

"Inter—"

"Nope."

"Fine." Tom folded his arms. "I would like a candy car. That is my final offer."

"A candy car!" Uncle Herbert looked so shocked that Kate laughed. "That's the most ridiculous thing I've ever heard!"

"Oh, come on!" Tom said. "It'd be awesome!"

"I'm kidding," Uncle Herbert said. "You can totally have a candy car. What else?"

"A swimming pool car!" Kate said. It was worth a try. Especially if candy cars were a thing.

"Why not."

"All right," she said. "Read that back."

"Two passenger cars," Uncle Herbert read.

"Two dining cars, two kitchen cars, sleeper car, library car, candy car, swimming pool car."

Two, four...ten cars. That seemed about right. Maybe a tiny bit short.

"Let's have a flat car," Tom said. "Like just plain. We can stand on it and pretend we're surfing. And we should have boxcars, too. Trains always have boxcars."

Uncle Herbert wrote on his clipboard.

"I think," Kate said, "we should have a mystery car. Like we don't know what's in it, but it's something cool."

She thought she was pushing her luck with that one, but he wrote it down with the rest.

"That's all I got," Kate said.

"Me too."

"Needs one more thing," Uncle Herbert said.

"What?"

"Come on. Every train has one."

"Oh—a caboose!"

"Now you're done." He turned to go.

"Uncle Herbert?" Tom looked like he had a thought that he was trying hard to formulate into a question. "Why are we here?"

"You mean here in the rail yard?"

"No, I mean—like why are we on a train in the middle of nowhere? Where are we going?"

It was a fair question. Kate wondered why she hadn't thought to ask it herself. She had the dizzy feeling of being caught up in something much larger than she'd realized—like she was a player in an enormous game that she didn't know the rules of yet, or like she'd happened to glance out the window of a building and discovered that she was much, much higher up than she'd realized.

"You're going on an adventure," Uncle Herbert said. "Isn't that what you wanted?"

"Yeah..."

Tom didn't look completely satisfied with that, but Uncle Herbert just waved the clipboard.

"I'll get this up to the dispatcher. Just remember: Keep the water tank full, and never let the fire go out. And keep an eye out for the twilight star."

He turned to go and then stopped again, peering up at them in the darkness. "Wait a second. Something's wrong. You look… floppy. Droopy."

His lack of experience with children was showing again.

"We're tired, Uncle Herbert," Kate said. "It's really late."

As soon as she'd said it, she yawned.

"Oh." He rubbed his chin. "That's right, probably it's past your bedtime. Why don't we hitch up the passenger cars and the sleeper car and you can go to bed."

"Like sleep here? On the train? What about Mom and Dad?"

"I'll explain it to them."

"They're going to go mental," Tom said. "You realize that. Like, they will literally take leave of their actual senses."

"Might be good for them," Uncle Herbert said. "They're much too sane, those two. Night-night."

With that he walked away, presumably to go find the dispatcher, whoever that was.

Suddenly Kate could barely keep her eyes open. She had no idea she was so exhausted.

It was late, and about two months' worth of stuff had happened to her in one day, and it was all catching up with her at once. She sat on her little fold-down seat and leaned against the wall and closed her eyes.

She wondered what Uncle Herbert had meant when he'd said that about magic. It was impossible. There was no such thing. But at the same time it didn't seem like the kind of thing you just *said*. And evidence to the contrary was mounting up like snow in a blizzard.

More wisdom from Grace Hopper floated through her mind: "If they put you down somewhere with nothing to do, go to sleep. You don't know when you'll get any more."

Kate couldn't have said how much time passed before she felt a gentle *bump. That must be the first passenger car being hitched up*, she thought, without opening her eyes. And then *bump*: passenger car number two.

I hope the animals will like them, she thought.

And then *bump: That must be the sleeper car.*

As if in a dream, she and Tom climbed down out of the cab. They barely even noticed the click-*bing* of the train saying

GOOD NIGHT

It was beyond strange, being out in the middle of the night in a rail yard that shouldn't have existed, in a winter that should've been summer, but Kate was too tired to care. The night air was freezing, and the ground was covered with a mix of snow and gravel that was extremely painful to walk on in bare feet. Train cars loomed over them, big as houses, casting sharp black shadows in the artificial light. Past the passenger cars they found the sleeper car.

It was painted a comforting cream color, like ivory or very fancy paper, and it had two doors, one at each end. The first door had TOM neatly lettered on it. The second said KATE. When Kate got to her door it opened automatically and clever little metal steps folded down. Much easier than getting into the engine.

Inside it was warm, and the lights were dim. On one wall was a little sink with a mirror over it. Next to that was a hook with a soft white towel hanging on it and a holder for an enamel cup with a toothbrush and toothpaste in it. Everything was ever-so-slightly miniaturized to fit in a train compartment. It was like being a doll in a very expensive dollhouse.

There was a closet, with a soft Kate-sized robe and slippers already in it and a little drawer for a pair of neatly folded blue-and-white-striped flannel pajamas. Whoever had put all this together was extremely well organized, Kate thought.

She was so tired she just splashed some water on her face and dried it with the towel. The pajamas felt cool and soft and clean. She didn't brush her teeth, because what was even the point of getting to sleep on a magic train if you had to brush your teeth?

There was a little bed that folded down from the wall, with a little bookshelf next to it in case you wanted to read before you went

to sleep. Which ordinarily she might have done, but not tonight. She was too tired even to read. She turned out the light, snugged the blanket up over her, and took a deep contented breath. The sleeper car smelled like clean linen and scented wood. There was a window over the bed so you could look up and see the stars.

A tiny door opened in one wall. Tom's face peered through it from the other half of the sleeper.

"Hey," he said.

"Pretty nice, right?"

"So awesome." Tom paused for a second. "Hey—is it okay if I leave this open?"

Sometimes she forgot that Tom was two years younger than she was. He'd never even been on a sleepover, except with their grandparents, and now he was going to sleep on a talking train in the middle of a mysterious rail yard.

It might even make her feel better too.

"Definitely okay. Good night, Tom."

"Good night."

Kate closed her eyes and slept.

Tickets, Please

KATE WOKE UP TO THE SOFT CLICKETY rhythm of a moving train. Morning sunlight streamed in through the little window of the sleeper car. She sat up. For a second she had no idea where she was.

Then it all came rushing back—her birthday, the train, Uncle Herbert, the animals, everything—so fast it made her head spin. She peered through the peephole into Tom's room. It was a mirror image of hers, except that it had Tom in it. He was still asleep.

Kate opened the window. The morning was

cold and clear and smelled like snowy woods. Ahead the *Silver Arrow* was puffing out gray smoke and white steam, and behind them a proper train stretched out now. The cars were all different colors: black and white and pine green and sky blue and brick red and bulldozer yellow. One of them, painted a deep indigo blue, was a yard taller than all the others.

She counted them: fifteen cars. Wherever they were going, they were going there in a real train.

There were clothes in the closet, which was good, because her old clothes were way too light for winter, which it now apparently was, and they weren't especially clean either. Though the new clothes were a little odd: a white blouse, thick gray cotton overalls, and a matching blazer. There was also an old-fashioned-looking

black winter coat made of waxed canvas, with interesting brass buttons, and a pair of excitingly grown-up-looking black steel-capped boots that would be exceptionally good for kicking people with, if for some reason that ever became necessary.

She put on the clothes, all except for the coat, and made her way back to the dining car. Or one of them, assuming there really were two.

A buffet was laid out for breakfast. She took scrambled eggs, granola and yogurt and some berries, bacon, toast with butter and peach jam— both bacon and toast were slightly charred, which happened to be how she liked them—plus a big glass of fresh orange juice. She felt kind of greedy taking all that, but it was made already, so she figured she might as well eat it.

She laid it all out on a table by a window, then she went back to the sleeper car and got a book from the little shelf over the bed. For a certain kind of person there is literally nothing nicer than eating breakfast by yourself on a moving train with a good book. Kate was one of those people.

She was feeling something—a new feeling. Not even a feeling exactly, more like she wasn't feeling a lot of things that she was used to feeling. She wasn't tired, or bored, or frustrated, or wishing she was somewhere else doing something else. All that was cleared away. She still had basically no idea what was going on, but she knew she was free to be herself, right here, right now, in the moment. She couldn't wait to find out what she was going to feel next.

The train slowed down. They were almost back at the station from last night. Tom came in, yawning, still in his pajamas, chewing on a piece of bacon.

"You think we're supposed to be doing something?" he said.

"Probably. Don't know what, though."

Click-*bing*!

There was another one of those scrolling pieces of paper in the dining car, right by the door. Kate hadn't noticed it before.

YES, YOU'RE SUPPOSED TO BE DOING
SOMETHING

"Well?" Tom said. "Do you want us to guess?"

THAT WOULD BE NICE BUT YOU'D ONLY GUESS WRONG

WE'RE COMING TO THE STATION

GO TO THE PASSENGER CARS AND TAKE THE PASSENGERS' TICKETS

"Oh."

That did make a certain kind of sense. And it didn't sound that hard. At least in theory.

In an alcove by the door to the passenger cars they found two conductor's hats, which somehow looked a lot less dorky now, and two of those mysterious metal hole-punchers that train conductors always have. Both hats had the words *The Silver Arrow* stitched on them in little letters.

Silently they placed the hats on their heads. Then they frowned and swapped hats. Better.

"Hey, how come you get a uniform?" Tom said.

If there was one thing Tom hated, it was when Kate got something and he didn't. It was childish and selfish, and Kate felt exactly the same way.

"It was in the closet in the sleeper car. Didn't you look?"

"No!"

Brakes squealed and the train stopped.

"Well, too late," she said. "You'll have to do it in your pajamas."

"Ugh!"

The doors opened. The platform was still full of animals, patiently waiting. She wondered if they'd been there all night. Maybe animals didn't get bored.

They began to file into the train.

Even by human standards they were incredibly polite. There was no pushing or shoving. No one barked or growled or squawked or tried to eat any of their fellow travelers, though Kate did notice that the larger and more predatory animals—a wolf, a bear, a couple of large owls—tended to sit in the forward carriage, and the smaller, fluffier, more vulnerable animals kept to the rear. They all had a light dusting of snow on their fur or feathers.

These weren't pets, or farm animals, or animals in a zoo, which always looked so dull and downcast and desperate. These were wild animals, and there was nothing between her and them—no fence, no glass, nothing. She could've reached out and touched them if she dared. It was almost like she was one of them.

As before, each animal held a single paper ticket in its mouth.

The cars were divided into old-fashioned train compartments, and one by one the animals settled into them. The foxes curled up neatly on the seats with their tails under their chins. The birds perched on the luggage racks and seat backs. The bigger animals had to sort of squash themselves in. Some of the very small, shy animals, like possums and rabbits, hid under the seats. Everybody kept well clear of a large, slow-moving porcupine.

A lot of cold air came in with them, and Kate shivered in her conductor's blazer—should've gone back for the winter coat, but

too late now. She waited till the train was moving again, then opened the door to the first compartment. It was occupied by a family of deer—a doe and a stag and a fawn—plus a somber, tattered-looking gray hawk. A crowd of mice huddled under the seat.

They all looked at her. Kate cleared her throat. She wished somebody had explained exactly what she was supposed to do and how to do it.

But what's the worst that could happen? They had tickets. She was going to take them.

"Tickets, please," Kate said.

The doe stretched her neck elegantly forward with all three of her family's tickets in her mouth. They had deer tooth marks on them, and the words HOWLAND FOREST were printed on them. She fumbled with the hole-puncher before she figured out how to work it, then she punched the tickets and handed them back.

It was actually very satisfying. She guessed the train must be going to Howland Forest. Wherever that was. She hoped the *Silver Arrow* knew.

Porcupine vs. Bird: Fight!

THE NEXT COMPARTMENT HELD MORE BIRDS, two turtles and something long and slinky and furry that she supposed was probably a weasel or something. A gigantic black bear had the compartment after that all to itself. The next one held a fat black-striped badger— the one she'd met earlier—and a family of spotted skunks, which were small but looked like they were afraid of literally nothing in the universe. Also a whole row of sleepy bats.

The tickets had all kinds of destinations printed on them: ISLE OF WIGHT, LOWER SILESIAN

WILDERNESS, SAGANO BAMBOO FOREST....
They sounded like they were from all over the world. Kate wondered why they could possibly be going to all those different places, and how they expected to get there on a steam train, but she didn't feel like she could ask. Her job was to punch the tickets, and she punched them.

She accepted a ticket from a largish feline—not a house cat or quite a big cat, but

something in between. Its fur was partly spotted and partly striped, and it was a funny color, gray with a hint of olive green.

"Thanks," it said.

"You're welcome."

Was it a bobcat? A lynx? Kate hadn't studied for this.

"It was brave of you to come," the something-cat said. "After what happened last time."

Kate gave it a funny look. Or she? She sounded like a she. And if animals were going to talk to her, she supposed she shouldn't think of them as *its*. Kate wanted to say that it wasn't really that brave, since she didn't know what had happened last time, and *wait-a-minute what are you even talking about?!* But she had a lot of tickets to take.

The last compartment contained more weasels—or were they minks? stoats?—that wouldn't or couldn't stop chasing each other in circles. There was also a big wild turkey and more bats and a wolf who looked like a demon in wolf form but was probably perfectly nice when you got to know her.

Then Kate was done. She took a deep breath and leaned back against the wall in the corridor. Whew. That went well.

At that exact moment a loud, excited chittering and squawking came from a compartment down the hall. Kate hurried over, straightening her conductor's hat. A striking white bird with a black cap and an orange beak was perched on the luggage rack, glaring down at the compartment's other occupant, which was the big porcupine.

"Get down from there!" the porcupine said. "Right now!"

"No."

"This is my compartment, you unbelievably unpleasant bird!"

"I don't see how my being here could inconvenience you even slightly!"

"If you don't get down right now, I will stand up on my hind legs and—"

"Porcupines can't stand on their hind legs," the bird said.

"We can! For brief periods!"

Though he didn't demonstrate.

"Look," the bird said, "if we just agree that the luggage rack and the upper edge of the seat backs are my domain, and—"

"Why don't we agree that *you'll* get out of *my* compartment right now or I'll quill you into next week!"

"I'm not even sure what that means," Kate said. "What's going on here?"

She had only just found out that animals could talk, and already she was wishing these two would shut up for a minute.

"I'll tell you what's going on," the porcupine said. "I have a special ticket for my own private compartment, and now this trash-eating seagull won't get out of it!"

The porcupine proudly displayed his ticket, which was stuck on the point of one of his spines.

"You are betraying your ignorance," said the bird. "I'm not a seagull. I'm a roseate tern."

"Well, good for you."

"It is good, thank you very much. And we

don't eat trash, we eat fish." He drew himself up with as much dignity as a roseate tern can muster. "We are plunge divers."

Kate examined the porcupine's ticket more closely.

"It says *where available*," she said. "That means you get your own compartment if we have one. But I'm not sure there are any empty compartments right now."

"This compartment would be empty," the

porcupine pointed out, "if you'd just get that bird out of it!"

"I don't have anywhere to put him," Kate said firmly.

"Put him in with the hawks."

"Hawks prey on terns," said the bird.

The porcupine shrugged. "Circle of life."

"It's not! It's the circle of death!"

Both animals looked at Kate. Incredibly, it seemed like they were waiting for her to settle the argument.

It was the kind of thing nobody ever asked her to do at home. At home there was always somebody else—a teacher, a parent, some-body. But here there was only her. She was going to have to think of something.

But what?

"Maybe," she said finally, to the porcupine, "you'd be more comfortable in our library car."

The Library Car

IT WAS A CALCULATED RISK. KATE HADN'T actually seen the library car yet, and she didn't know exactly where it was. She wasn't even 100 percent sure it existed. But it was the only thing she could think of.

"Library car." The porcupine considered it. Then he sighed, as if library cars were an indignity that he suffered on a daily basis. "Oh, all right. If we must!"

The porcupine's white-tipped quills swayed stiffly from side to side as he waddled past Kate and out into the corridor. She followed him. Though not too closely. On their way they passed Tom, still in his pajamas.

"Why don't you head on up to the engine," she said. "See if the train needs more coal."

She had no idea if Tom was going to do what she said. Most of the time when she told Tom to do something, he either did nothing or the exact opposite. But now he just nodded and headed forward.

Look at that. She could get used to this conducting business.

Kate and the porcupine walked back along the swaying, rumbling, *chuff-chuff*ing train, through the sleeper car, then the dining car, then the kitchen car, then the other kitchen car, then the other dining car. Kate was starting to get a little nervous when they finally opened the door to the library car.

All credit to Uncle Herbert: It was not a disappointment.

This was the extra-tall indigo-colored car she'd seen earlier. Every square inch of its walls was crammed with books—the shelves ran all the way up to the ceiling, which must

have been fifteen feet high. There were even bookshelves over the doors and windows. The floor was covered in thick red oriental rugs, and there were two overstuffed leather armchairs and a big, long, comfy couch. It even smelled like a library.

OMG, Kate thought. *I am awesome at inventing train cars!*

The porcupine looked around.

"It'll do."

He climbed up onto one of the armchairs, settled down, and closed his eyes.

"I'm mostly nocturnal," he explained.

Then he went to sleep.

Kate walked the length of the library car, running her fingertips over the spines of the books. Each bookshelf had a wooden bar along it to keep the books from falling off when the train swayed; you could unlatch it and swing it open to get a book out. It was exactly what she'd imagined, only more so.

She skimmed a few titles. It was an incredibly random bunch of books: fat, dignified old hardcovers; big, skinny picture books; cheap paperbacks with spines so worn that you couldn't read the titles anymore. There were guides to identifying moths in distant parts of the world, and multivolume sets of the complete letters of people with long, unpronounceable names, and romance novels with heroines spilling out of their gowns and heroes busting out of their shirts, and thrillers and horror stories with creepy one-word titles like *The Trees* and

The Leaves, and important grown-up novels that she mentally reminded herself to skim later for interesting and/or bad words.

And every once in a while, like a friendly face in a crowd, there were the kinds of books that Kate liked, which fell into two general categories: books about science and books about ordinary people who find out that magic is real.

Kate took down a promising-looking book from the second category and sat on the couch with it. Twenty minutes later, when the hero of the novel was just at the point of discovering that the horrible, abusive private school he'd been transferred to after the unexplained deaths of his parents had a secret school *underneath* it, accessible via the locker of that one kid who had mysteriously disappeared last year, something alerted her to the fact that she was being watched.

It was the cat—the one she'd met before, who was neither a big cat nor a small cat. She must have come in without Kate hearing. Her head had dramatic black stripes, almost like a badger's. Kate really wanted to know what kind of cat she was.

"Sorry," Kate said. "I didn't see you there."

"I saw you there," the cat said.

"For a second I thought you were a pillow."

"For a second I thought you were a large, defenseless rodent."

Kate wondered if she should be a little worried. She was definitely bigger than the cat, but she wouldn't have wanted to get into a fight with her.

"I guess I was really caught up in this book I'm reading," Kate said carefully.

"It must be very good."

"It's all right. There's a lot of description. I've been skimming a little. Have you read it?"

"No," the cat said. "I'm not here for the books."

"Oh. Why are you here?"

"To be alone. We're not social animals."

Kate wondered if that was a hint that she should leave. But she was here first. And it was her train. She tried to keep things going instead.

"What kind of cat are you? If you don't mind my asking."

"I don't mind. I'm a fishing cat."

"Sorry, but does that mean you're a cat who likes to fish? Or is there an actual kind of cat called a fishing cat?"

"The second one." She began licking a large paw. "I'm not surprised you haven't heard of us. There aren't many of us, and we don't get as much attention as the big cats. We're related to the rusty-spotted cats and the flat-headed cats—unfortunate name that, although it's true, they have very flat heads. And they eat *fruit,* if you can believe it. A cat that eats fruit! Also the leopard cats."

"Oh. Are leopard cats the same as leopards?"

"No."

There was another lull. Kate tried to think of something more to say. It was hard to tell what the cat was thinking. Though she guessed that was true of every cat ever.

"So—what's it like being a fishing cat?"

"Oh, you know. We live in swamps and

mangrove forests. We hunt. We swim. And we fish, obviously."

"Wait, you swim? Like, in water?"

"Absolutely!" It was the first topic the fishing cat sounded really enthusiastic about. "We love it. Other cats think it's weird, but we don't care. I mean, it's not like we eat fruit!"

"I can't believe you swim!"

"Well, I don't like to boast about it. Tigers do it, too. But fishing cats probably do it the most. We have waterproof fur. And look." She held up a paw. "Our toes are even a little bit webbed."

"That is so amazing!"

The cat seemed pleased.

"You said something before, about what happened last time," Kate said. "With the train. What did you mean?"

"Oh, I thought they would've told you about that," the cat said. "As part of your training."

"But that's the thing, I didn't get trained! At all!"

Maybe she shouldn't have admitted that, but it just came out.

"Is that right? How extraordinary." The fishing cat flopped her heavy tail from side to side like a velvet rope. "Well, it was before my time—we live only ten or fifteen years, you know. But I do know that before this train there was another one, and it left one day and never came back. I don't know what happened to it, but I doubt it was anything good."

Just then the door opened and two more animals came in.

One was a very long, very thin snake with large, alert black eyes and skin so bright green it was almost fluorescent. Kate felt a powerful instinctive urge to run away from it very, very fast. The other was some kind of large wading bird with long legs and a curvy neck. If pressed Kate might've said it was a stork. Or a heron. Or a crane? Or were they all the same thing? You think you know something about animals, and then you have to conduct a whole train full of them. Anyway, it was a big fancy bird. Not the kind you see every day.

"Mind if we join you?" the bird said. She had a lot of long, elegant gray feathers.

"Yes," said the cat.

"That'sssssssss too bad," the snake said, sliding smoothly inside. "It'ssssssss because I'm venomoussssss, I know."

He slithered up onto a chair.

"It'sssssss a common prejudiccccccce."

(I'm not going to keep typing all the extra *s*'s, so just keep in mind that the snake hisses a lot when he talks.)

"A library car," the heron said. "This is fantastic. Who would've thought?"

Kate glowed quietly inside: *She* would've thought!

With two beats of her enormous wings the heron flew up to perch on a lamp.

"You always say things are fantastic," the snake scoffed.

"Well, you never do," she said, "so I have to do it twice as much. And anyway, it is!" She turned to Kate. "Are there any cars with fish in them?"

"I was wondering that, too," the fishing cat said.

"There's no fish car," Kate said. Like she would have a fish car! "But they might serve fish in one of the dining cars."

The porcupine woke up and squinted sleepily at the cat, the bird, the snake, and the human.

"I thought I would be alone in here," he said.

"And now we're here!" the heron said. "Isn't it fantastic?"

"I would like everybody to be clear," the porcupine said, "that I have approximately thirty thousand quills on my body. They're mostly for defense, but believe me, they can be lethal."

The other animals looked at one another.

"I don't know about all of you, but I'm very frightened." The fishing cat rolled onto her back on the couch, paws in the air, and stretched exactly like a house cat would. She didn't look very frightened.

"Me too," the snake said. "I would shut my eyes in terror, but I don't have any eyelids."

"Really?" Kate said. "How is that possible?"

"I have a transparent scale over each eye. Much more elegant than eyelids."

"But don't you ever want to close your eyes?"

"Not really," the snake said. "I do like licking them, though."

"I don't want to brag," the heron said, "but I have three eyelids."

"Wait, what?!" Kate said.

"It's true! Upper eyelid, lower eyelid, plus a nictitating membrane."

"I'm not even listening," said the snake. "Because I also don't have any ears. Or a nose. I smell with my tongue."

Animals were a lot weirder than Kate had realized.

"I am very much wishing that I had never evolved ears right now," the porcupine said.

"Maybe you could read a book," Kate said brightly. "Lots of good books here in the library car!"

"That would be nice," the cat said, "but we can't read."

Click-*bing*.

SORRY TO INTERRUPT THIS FASCINATING

CONVERSATION

BUT DUTY CALLS

The train was slowing down again. They were coming to another station.

"I'd better go." Kate stood up, kind of relieved. "It was nice meeting you all."

She slipped out. Though honestly she was

worried that they would all kill one another if they weren't supervised.

As an afterthought, she wondered who would win if they *did* all have a fight. She thought it would probably be the porcupine.

The Baby That Looked Like a Pine Cone

THE LANDSCAPE OUTSIDE WAS CHANGING. they'd left the winter forest behind and entered what looked more like a tropical jungle. When Kate opened a door and looked out—which was kind of awesome all on its own, sticking your head out the open door of a moving train without getting yelled at by the conductor *because the conductor was you*—the air was warm and humid and smelled like an incredible wealth of green life.

The station platform was overgrown with vines and ferns and littered with giant leaves.

Palm trees crowded around it, and green shoots pushed up between the railroad ties. Waiting on the platform were an iguana, two large snakes, a couple of amazing golden-haired monkeys that looked like they'd had their faces spray-painted pink, and something like a small hippo with a big nose that she thought might be a tapir. Plus some colorful glossy frogs that looked like pieces of candy.

The air was full of burbling, shrieking birdsong, and a gorgeous translucent-green light showered down through the trees. The sign on the platform read TUMUCUMAQUE, which much later Kate would figure out was in the Amazon.

Kate thought she'd better announce the name of the station, the way they did on regular trains, though she had no idea how to pronounce it. She said it several times in different ways just to be sure. She must've gotten it right at least once because a few animals quietly left their compartments and trotted and slithered and fluttered out into the heat of the jungle.

Kate grabbed a banana from the dining car

before the next stop, which was in a bamboo grove. The station after that was giant redwoods, and after that was a dusty plain where a brutal sun beat down. It was so hot she had to take off her blazer.

Only two hardy wild dogs got on there, and one very small tortoise that took what seemed like half an hour to cross the platform. Kate felt like she was starting to get the hang of this, whatever this was, enough that she had some spare energy to start wondering about the big picture. As soon as she did, a million questions started asking themselves in her head. How could a giant steam train go to all these places? Why did nobody else know about this? Was the train invisible? And who put down all these tracks? Who sold all these animals their tickets? And so on. In a way she didn't want to ask, because she was afraid that doing so might disturb some fragile enchantment, and it would all turn out to be a dream and evaporate as mysteriously as it had arrived.

She just wanted it to keep on going. But at

the same time she knew that sooner or later those questions would need answering.

The next stop was another rain forest. When all the other animals had gotten on and off the train, there was one left on the platform all by itself.

At first Kate wasn't completely sure it was an animal. It looked more like a pine cone. It was tiny and brown and round, with pointy overlapping scales. But when she looked closer, she saw that it had four legs and a tail and a little face. It was curled up tightly, its eyes shut, fast asleep.

Touching unidentified wild animals with her bare hands was not a thing Kate was completely comfortable with. But she could also see that, clutched tightly to the creature's little belly, in its two clawed front paws, was a ticket.

And it looked so helpless. It was just a baby, and it was all alone.

She sighed. She even said the word out loud:

"Sigh."

She picked up the little animal, cupping it gently in her two hands, praying it wouldn't bite her or scratch her or go to the bathroom on her, and quickly carried it inside. Its scales were dry and scratchy. The train started up again.

Kate took it back to the library. She couldn't think what else to do with it. The porcupine, the cat, the heron, and the snake were all still arguing, but they stopped when she came in.

"Okay," she said. "Does anybody know what this is?"

The cat peered at it. "It looks like a pine cone."

"That's what I thought," Kate said.

"Or an artichoke," the cat said.

"It's not. It's some kind of animal."

"That," the heron said, "is a baby pangolin."

"I don't know everything," Kate said, "but I think I know what a penguin looks like."

"Not a penguin, a pangolin. It's the only mammal in the world with scales. Pangolins are incredibly rare."

"Awesome." Kate placed it carefully on a cushion on the couch. "Congratulations on your new baby pangolin. Take good care of it."

She left before anybody could object. Then she went forward to check on Tom and the engine.

Tom was alive and well, but extremely sweaty and almost completely covered in coal dust.

"Might be time to hit the swimming pool car," Kate said.

"Click," he said. "Bing."

Click-*bing*!

IT'S GOING WELL THANK YOU

BUT I'M A LITTLE LOW ON FUEL

She'd almost forgotten that the train could talk. There's a lot going on in your life when you have more urgent things to think about than a talking train.

"Low on fuel. Okay, that sounds important." She seemed to remember Uncle Herbert saying something about that. "Can I help?"

NOT YET

WE'LL HAVE TO STOP FOR IT
SOMEWHERE SOON THOUGH

One of the things Kate was learning on the train was what to do when you saw a problem, which was that you tried to solve it. At home her usual approach to a problem was to ignore it till her parents noticed it, at which point they would solve it for her—but here on the train there were no parents. She was in charge.

Not solving problems was way easier than solving them, obviously. But left to their own devices, problems usually only got worse. Better to get it over with.

In the meantime they had their next train

lesson. The *Silver Arrow* talked Kate and Tom through the process of getting the engine going from a standing start. The train was right about one thing: It was a good teacher. It taught them how to read the steam pressure gauge and the little glass tube that showed the water level in the boiler. They went over the brakes and the throttle again, and it introduced them to a mysterious but important device called a reversing lever, which controlled how much steam power went to the pistons.

Or something like that.

"I thought that's what the throttle did," Kate said.

IT'S—WELL—THINK OF IT LIKE THE
GEARBOX ON A CAR

"I don't know how that works either."

OKAY, THE GEARS ON A BICYCLE—WAIT

HMMM

"Hmmm?" Tom said. "What's 'hmmm'?"

THERE'S A STATION COMING UP

"Okay..."

BUT IT'S NOT ON THE SCHEDULE

"Can I actually see the schedule?" Kate said.

NO

"Well, what should we do?"

DON'T ASK ME. YOU'RE THE CONDUCTOR

Kate thought of saying, *Well, you're the train!* or *How am I supposed to know?* or maybe *But Tom's a conductor, too!* But she didn't. She couldn't, really. She hadn't asked to be the conductor of a magic steam train, or not exactly, but deep down she knew she kind of had. She'd wanted something real, something that wasn't kid stuff. Something that mattered. And looky here, this was it.

And Uncle Herbert had told her to get off the train, right at the start, and she hadn't. If she wasn't sure what to do, she would just have to guess based on what she did know and live with the consequences.

Probably that was an important life lesson she was supposed to be learning from this whole experience. Which was fine, she guessed, though she hoped there weren't too many more of them.

"Okay, let's stop," she said. "Let's find out what's going on."

Kate Finds Out
What's Going On

SO THEY THROTTLED THE *SILVER ARROW* DOWN, and fiddled with the reversing lever, and applied the brakes, and Kate took her ticket-puncher and straightened her conductor's hat and went back to the passenger cars.

They were chugging through a pine forest now, and the air smelled pleasantly like their garage had after the time Kate spilled turpentine there. They pulled up at a plain cement platform, and Kate threw the big brass lever that opened the doors.

Something was different. Usually there was

a sign on the platform saying where they were, but this time Kate couldn't see one anywhere.

Six or seven gray squirrels, a huge gray pig, and a couple of brown snakes waited on the platform. On the ground and the branches overhead sat a whole flock of black birds with a slight iridescent rainbow shine to their wings that reminded Kate of an oil slick.

She recognized the birds. They were sparrows—or no, not sparrows, starlings! That's what they were. None of the creatures moved. They just sat there staring at her.

Then she realized that something else was different, too. None of them were holding tickets.

"So...hi," Kate said.

The giant pig trotted forward and stood right in front of her. He really was unbelievably big, as tall as she was, and he looked much more fit somehow than your average pig. In fact, he seemed to be completely made out of muscle.

That's not a pig at all, Kate thought. *That must be a wild boar.* She'd never seen one in

real life. He had tiny eyes and a wet nose and huge upward-thrusting yellow tusks.

Kate cleared her throat. "Tickets, please."

The boar just stood there in front of her. She tried again.

"I'm sorry, but you can't ride the train without a ticket."

"I don't have a ticket," the boar said in a deep voice.

"Well," Kate said slowly, "I guess you can't ride the train, then."

"Then I guess we have a problem."

Kate frowned. She wasn't immediately warming to this boar.

"I am sorry to have to say this," she said, "but it more seems like *you* have a problem."

"You don't sound very sorry," chittered a squirrel.

So that's how it's going to be, Kate thought. She folded her arms with more firmness than she really felt.

"I really am sorry, but I don't make the rules. If it's that important, why don't you just go and get tickets and come back? I'm sure we'll be back here soon."

That was a fib—she wasn't sure at all—but she really wanted to bring this conversation to an end. She stepped back into the train and closed the doors.

But the doors didn't close, because the boar stuck his huge head right in between them. He had large, furry ears and not the slightest trace of a neck.

"I don't want a ticket," he said. "I want to get on this train. Now be a good girl and open the door."

They stared at each other. He didn't seem to be even the slightest bit bothered by having the doors closed on his head. Kate thought about it: Really, who would it hurt if she let them on? It's not like she needed their money. (If animals even had money. She wondered again how exactly they got their tickets.) Plus this boar weighed about five times what she did and could probably kill her in about ten seconds, even taking into account the awesome kicking power of her new steel-capped boots.

One of the brown snakes pushed forward between the boar's hooves.

"Look, I can see you're in a tough position." The snake's voice was calm and reasonable and almost sympathetic. "You're on a tight schedule. You have to get this train moving. But thing is, we've got all day, and we're not going to let this train go till you let us on. You can't win, so why not just let it slide and we'll all be on our way?"

"Trust us," a squirrel said, "you don't want to make an issue out of this."

It would've been so easy to give in—giving in was almost always the easiest thing, in Kate's experience. The only problem was—what was the problem? It felt wrong. This was her train. Uncle Herbert had given it to her, and it was the first thing ever that was well and truly her responsibility. It came with rules, and the rule was that you had to have a ticket. Maybe it was a stupid rule, but that was up to her, not these animals. It was time to decide whether she was going to let herself be bullied.

And when she realized that, she realized that she'd already decided.

"But I don't trust you. Not in the slightest." She wished her voice weren't shaking, but it was. "And I'm not making an issue out of this, it's already an issue. Get off my train, please. Right now."

Kate pointed in the direction of "off the

train," in case that made it clearer. She stared into the boar's tiny orange eyes. She wished Tom were there.

The boar didn't move. Instead he snorted at her:

"RONK!"

The sound was deafening—like an explosion. She jumped three feet backward out of sheer terror.

"RONK RONK RONK RONK RONK!"

Kate had gotten so used to animals talking politely that she'd almost forgotten they were wild creatures. They weren't tame. They weren't safe. The boar strained at the doors to get at her. He tossed his head viciously, with those tusks, and Kate cowered back even farther. She'd thought she wanted this—she'd thought she wanted an adventure—but she hadn't thought at all about how scary it would be! She hadn't thought about the fact that when you were in it, you didn't know how it would end! For all you knew you could end up gored and trampled by an angry boar far from home and never see your parents again—

"What on earth do you think you're doing? Get your fat head out of those doors!"

The voice came from behind Kate.

Kate didn't dare take her eyes off the boar. But as she watched, an incredible thing happened to him. The boar's little eyes went as wide as they could go, and his huge, snorting face showed an expression Kate hadn't thought it was capable of.

It was fear. Kate risked a glance behind her. The voice belonged to the porcupine.

His black-and-white danger-striped quills were rattling and sticking up from his body in a huge, ridiculous ruff. It was like a deadly case of bedhead. He was rude, and sulky, and thoroughly unpleasant, and Kate had never been so glad to see anyone in her whole life.

The porcupine took a step forward. The boar took a step backward—and Kate slammed the doors shut in his big, fat face.

The engine chuffed. The train pulled out of the station. Kate's knees felt weak. She sank down onto the floor.

"Thank you," she said.

"You're welcome."

"I did not want him on this train!" She hugged herself.

"You were right," the porcupine said. "He didn't belong here."

The porcupine's quills were lying back down. He must be able to control them, she thought.

"I'm just glad I didn't have to quill him," he said, perfectly calmly. "Takes weeks to grow back a good quill."

"Does it hurt? When you use one?"

"A little. Like having a hair pulled out. Now, why don't you come with me to the dining car? You look pale. I'll bet you haven't had any lunch."

The Station That Wasn't There

WHEN KATE GOT TO THE DINING CAR, SHE was amazed to see the other animals from the library—the fishing cat, the green snake, and the heron—all sitting around a table together, chatting away like old friends. Apparently they'd bonded over the baby pangolin.

He was still asleep, but they'd made a nest for him in a fruit bowl. They were cooing over him and taking turns stroking him.

"Everything all right?" the heron said.

"Fine. No thanks to any of you." The porcupine was impressively unruffled by his

confrontation with the boar. Kate supposed that getting into fights with people was probably something that happened to him on a fairly routine basis. "How's the baby?"

"Fantastic! This is absolutely the cutest non-heron baby I have ever seen!"

"Shh!" the snake hissed. "You'll wake him."

Kate still found herself putting as much distance as politeness would allow between herself and the snake.

"How do you know he's a him?" Kate said.

All the animals stared at her.

"She can't tell," the snake hissed.

"It must be an animal thing," said the heron.

"Humans are animals," Kate said a little defensively.

"Of course you are," the fishing cat said. "But you've spent so much time pretending you're not, you've lost the knack."

The heron tactfully changed the subject. "Did you know that baby pangolins are called pangopups?" she said.

"That's a stupid name," the snake hissed.

"They should call them pangolings," the fishing cat said. "Or pangolini!"

"Baby porcupines are called porcupettes," the porcupine said with a shudder of disgust. "I don't see why humans think they get to name everything. They're not even very good at it. Electric eels—they're not even eels. In Australia there's a spider called a sparklemuffin!"

"And what about hellbenders?" the snake said. "Do they bend hell? Not even slightly."

"I wish I were called a hellbender," the cat said. "It's such a wonderful name. Wasted on a salamander."

"I don't understand what just happened." Kate still felt shaky. "Who were those animals out there?"

"Them?" the porcupine said. "Those were invaders."

"What were they invading, the train?"

The animals all exchanged a look.

"It's like this," the heron said. "As an animal, you have a place where you live and a place in the order of things. You prey on somebody, somebody else preys on you. It's not always pretty, but it keeps everything in balance.

"But sometimes an animal leaves its place in the world and goes somewhere else. Somewhere where it doesn't fit in. Often it just dies there because the climate's wrong or there's nothing for it to eat—but every once in a while it lucks into a situation where it has lots of things to prey on, and there's nobody to prey on it. What do you think happens then?"

"I don't know," Kate said. "It gets really fat and happy and dies of old age?"

"It eats everything in sight! Its population explodes till it's the only thing left!"

"Oh. So those animals who tried to get on the train were trying to do that?"

"Exactly."

"It's just bad form," the snake said. "I hope you quilled them."

"I should have!" the porcupine said.

"But some of them—I mean, they were just starlings," Kate said. "You know. Little birdies!"

Everybody hissed and growled and squawked at this.

"Let me tell you a story about starlings!" the porcupine said. "Starlings originally came from Europe. That's where they're supposed to live. But then some nitwit got it into his head that North America should have every bird species mentioned in the works of Shakespeare."

"Who's Shakespeare?" the fishing cat asked.

"That is actually kind of a cool idea," Kate said.

"No, it isn't! It isn't 'cool'! It was a catastrophe! This nitwit released sixty European starlings in New York City, and they mated and bred, and now they're all over America. There are two hundred million of them!"

"Okay, but what about those squirrels, though?" Kate said. "Little furry gray squirrels!"

"Oh, they went the other way round," the porcupine said. "Gray squirrels are from America. But then a tourist brought a few home to England because he thought they'd look nice on his country estate. Nice! They have a high old time in England. They eat birds, they kill trees, and they've driven the native red squirrels practically to extinction."

Kate thought about that. It didn't seem like anybody involved had had such bad intentions, really. They were small gestures. She still thought the Shakespeare thing sounded cool. But then look at what had happened! Everything that was so neatly balanced was ruined. Couldn't they send the animals back where they'd come from and start over? she wondered. More carefully this time? But how would you catch two hundred million starlings? She doubted she could even catch one.

Or a squirrel. There was no going back. The balance was lost forever.

She sighed. At any rate, she could keep them off her train.

"So what are all the other animals doing here?" she asked. "The ones who have tickets. How do you get tickets, anyway?"

"Oh, they just appear," the heron said. "I found mine in my nest when I came back from hunting."

"Mine was inside a fish," said the cat. "I almost ate it."

"My ticket was growing from a tree, like a leaf," said the snake. "Whoever runs the trains must issue them. Or maybe the tickets just issue themselves."

"But why?" Kate asked. "I mean, why do you need them? You're not invaders, are you?"

"Course not." Suddenly the heron sounded oddly embarrassed. "We're just—you know. We're migrating. That sort of thing. You know how we animals do that."

Something about the silence that followed made Kate wonder if she was really getting the whole story. But the train was slowing down again.

"All right," Kate said. "Excuse me, I think the train needs conducting."

Walking forward to the passenger cars, she looked out the window and got a shock: The train was now traveling over open water. Miles and miles of gray waves, with no land anywhere. The air was cold and tasted like salt, and she put her conductor's blazer back on, then went and got the winter coat too.

The train slowed and stopped, right there in the middle of the ocean. She looked around for a station, but there was nothing except water. Swells sloshed around the train's wheels. Was it a mistake? Had they overshot the platform somehow? She leaned out as far as she could and looked forward, then back. Nothing.

A chilly wind ruffled her hair. She could see her breath in the air.

And what were the train tracks resting on? She looked down but she couldn't see that, either. Pontoons? Some kind of underwater ridge? She had that same creepy feeling she had at the last stop: Something was off here.

We should go, she thought. She closed the doors—but as soon as the train started again, she heard a shout.

"Wait!" It was Tom, somewhere way down at the other end. "Wait! Stop the train!"

What now? Leaning out, she could see him standing on the flat car, waving frantically and pointing at something in the water. Kate ran back to join him.

He was crouched down, peering over the edge of the flat car into the ocean, so Kate looked too.

"I just saw it," he said. "A second ago."

"What?"

He shook his head. "I don't know. It was—"

Something big and white came rushing up at them from underwater. Kate was so shocked she fell over backward. For a second she was sure it was a great white shark leaping out of the water to devour them both in one mouthful.

But that didn't happen. It wasn't a shark. It was a polar bear.

The poor thing looked exhausted—she was desperately paddling to keep her black nose above the water. With the last of her strength, the bear lunged upward and got her head and paws onto the edge of the car.

Kate and Tom grabbed double handfuls of her cold, thick, wet fur and pulled as hard as

they could. The bear managed to get a hind foot onto the car, and Kate pulled on that, too. They heaved and heaved, and for a good minute there it felt like the poor thing would never make it, but finally the bear rolled and scraped and lumbered the rest of her body up onto the flat car, and all three of them collapsed, breathing hard.

Kate's shin burned where she'd skinned it

on the edge of the car. The polar bear was sopping wet, and even though she was incredibly heavy, she looked strangely thin for a bear. You could practically see her ribs. She didn't move. Kate wasn't even sure she was alive.

"I sure hope you have a ticket," she said.

Tom Was Right

KATE RAN OFF TO THE PASSENGER CARS TO recruit any animals who might be strong enough to help move the polar bear. She came back with a mountain lion, a couple of fellow bears, and a squad of very determined badgers, and together they rolled the polar bear onto a blanket and dragged her into the shelter of an empty boxcar. It probably would've been impossible if the poor thing hadn't been half-starved.

She did have a ticket, though, clamped in her powerful jaws.

Kate very carefully extracted it and punched it. She couldn't help but think that something had gone badly wrong here, but she wasn't sure exactly what. She got some towels and more blankets from the sleeper car, and together she and Tom dried the bear and got her as warm as they could. Finally Kate fetched a heaping bucket of fish and a big bowl of water from the kitchen and left them on a tray by the bear's head for when she woke up.

Kate put a wary hand on the polar bear's cold shoulder. Her fur was coarse and wiry.

"You'll be okay," she said. "You're safe now."

She hoped it was true.

By then it was dinnertime, and she went to the dining car to eat with the gang from the library. Tom came, too. The mood was subdued.

"I hope she'll be all right," Kate said.

"Sure she will," the heron said.

"Polar bears are tough," said the cat. "Very hard to kill."

"I could probably kill a polar bear," the

snake said. "Couldn't eat one, though, so what would be the point?"

Everybody stared at her.

"Anyway, she'll probably be fine."

It occurred to Kate that they hadn't all been properly introduced, not the way humans did it anyway. So she and Tom told the animals a little about themselves and where they came from, and the animals told her and Tom about themselves, too.

The snake was an eastern green mamba from South Africa. ("Another ridiculous name. Mamba—I can hardly say it! Only a creature with lips would think of a name like that.") He spent most of his time in trees. He insisted that in spite of his fearsome reputation he was rather shy and generally kept to himself.

The bird was a white-bellied heron from a river in India, and she was about a yard tall and incredibly beautiful—her neck was long and curvy, and her feathers were a million fine shades of gray. She had a thin, rather tasteful silvery crest on the top of her head, and, as advertised, a pure-white belly.

"We used to be called great Indian herons, or imperial herons," she said. "Come to think of it, I can't think why we changed. Those both sound much better."

Kate took the opportunity to ask her about something that had always bothered her, which was how herons could walk with knees that bent backward. It turned out that the heron's knees worked exactly the same way human knees did, you just couldn't see them because they were tucked up under her feathers. What looked like the heron's knee was actually her ankle, and what looked like her lower leg was actually a long, skinny foot.

Kate found that explanation almost equally unsettling.

"I always thought if I ever went on an adventure with talking animals, it would be with bunnies and mice and that sort of thing," Kate said. "I mean, no offense."

"None taken," said the porcupine (who was just a very grumpy North American porcupine from Michigan). "Though you're lucky.

Rabbits and mice are incredibly boring. All they talk about is vegetables and seeds."

For dinner the heron and the cat both ate fish. The porcupine worked his way through a big heap of clover, then gnawed on a branch. The mamba didn't eat at all.

"I swallowed a wild gerbil a few days ago," he explained, "and I'm still digesting. Besides, the sight of a mamba feeding is too awe-inspiring for most animals to watch."

"It's probably the way you inject your prey with horrible venom," the porcupine said, "that makes them suffocate in their own skin."

"Oh, that's only the beginning!" the mamba said. "Mamba venom also causes dizziness, nausea, difficulty swallowing, heart palpitations, and convulsions! Though it's true, it's usually the suffocation that does them in."

"Well, I think it's horrible."

"You're just jealous," the snake said, "because you can't shoot poison out of your teeth."

At this point Kate excused herself to go to bed. She was as tired as she could ever remember being, and she wanted to find a Band-Aid for her shin. And she was worried about the polar bear. And the invader animals. And the train was still short of fuel. When all this started she'd thought it was just going to be one big thrill ride, and it kind of was, but adventures were turning out to be a lot of hard work, too. And kind of stressful.

Tom headed the other way, toward the back of the train.

"The sleeper car's this way," Kate said.

"I know," Tom said. "But the candy car is this way."

Kate had almost forgotten about the candy car. She was tired—but you could never be too tired for candy.

Kate wasn't sure where it was, but it turned out that while she was hanging out in the library Tom had—with his usual surplus of energy—been off exploring the whole train from front to back. From the outside the candy car looked like an ordinary red metal boxcar, even a little on the rusty side—inside it was full of bright light and rainbow colors.

A wave of cool air rolled out, heavy with the smell of sugar. The walls were lined floor to ceiling with polished wooden shelves, and every inch of every shelf was loaded with candy. It was like Aladdin's cave crossed with the candy counter at a supermarket and multiplied by a million.

There were bundles of lollipops, and coils of black and red licorice ropes, and barrels of caramel cubes and fruit chews and sours and mints and nut clusters and brittles and candy canes and gobstoppers and honeycombs and gumballs and Swedish Fish. There were heaps of marshmallows and hard candies, and armies of gummy bears, and fields of candy corn. Candy necklaces hung from the ceiling.

There was a machine where you could type any flavor and it would deliver that flavor of jelly beans, by the pound. There was every candy bar ever made. Above all there was chocolate: milk chocolate, white chocolate, dark chocolate, solid bricks and bars of it wrapped in silver and gold foil. There were trays and trays of chocolates stuffed with

caramel and cherries and nuts and nougat and coconut and toffee and cream and pretzels and everything else you could imagine and a lot of things you couldn't.

It was all arranged by size and type and flavor and color, as neatly and carefully as a library. And it was all free, and it was all theirs.

"You laughed when I asked for a candy car," Tom said.

"I know."

"You thought it was funny."

"Whatever! You were right! Don't rub it in!" She hated when Tom was right. But if he had to be right about something, she was glad it was this. "Come on, let's see if we can eat one of everything. Except the coconut ones. Those are all yours." She hated coconut almost as much as she hated Tom being right.

But that night she never even made it past the chocolates, and Tom got stuck trying to stump the jelly bean machine till he couldn't eat any more.

Afterward they walked back together, happy, not talking, knowing that their cozy sleeping car was waiting for them, stopping only at the boxcar to make sure the polar bear was warm and sleeping peacefully. The train was chugging along beside a mountain lake as flat and smooth as glass. At home there were always streetlights around to spoil the night sky, but now, far away from the cities and suburbs, Kate and Tom really saw for the first time in their lives the blazing-white Milky Way spilling out across the deep black sky, which was perfectly reflected in the black mirror of the lake.

Uncle Herbert had said something before about a twilight star. She wondered if he'd meant one of these.

Then she went to bed. If the world were a just and fair place, she and Tom probably would've gotten stomachaches, but they didn't. Every once in a while the world is unfair in a good way.

The Branch Line

THE NEXT MORNING WHEN KATE WOKE UP
they were moving more slowly because the train
was heading uphill, into mountains.

The cat and the mamba and the heron and
the porcupine played with the baby pangolin. He'd finally woken up and was drinking
milk from a bottle. They'd made a new, even
more luxurious nest for him in a big salad
bowl from the kitchen lined with a soft, thick
towel. He was unbelievably cute for something whose entire body was basically covered
in fingernails.

The polar bear was still asleep, but the fish and the water Kate left for her were gone. That was a good sign: She'd eaten and drunk. Kate left her more of both, then went forward to the engine to check on the *Silver Arrow*.

They were crossing a steep slope covered with thin grass and gray rocks. Powdery snow fell out of a gray sky, and she picked up her heavy black coat from the sleeper car on the way forward.

But cold as it was outside, it was still warm in the cab. She breathed in the smell of steam and coal smoke and hot metal.

"How's it going?" she asked.

HUNGRY

NEED MORE FUEL

Right. It had said that before. She checked the tender, and it was getting pretty empty, just a few piles of coal left in the corners.

"Do you know where we can get more?"

MAYBE

"Maybe? How can you not know?!"

THERE'S NOTHING ON THE MAIN LINE

**WE'LL HAVE TO TRY A BRANCH LINE
INSTEAD**

"Okay. Is that bad?"

WE'LL FIND OUT

**THE BRANCH LINES ARE NOT WELL
EXPLORED**

"Well, I guess we'll explore them!"

There she went, looking on the bright side. She was as bad as Tom.

An hour or so later they came to a fork in the tracks and stopped. Kate and Tom climbed down from the engine and walked a few yards ahead to where a branch line peeled off to the right. There was a big iron lever by the side of the tracks that shunted trains from one line to another. They pulled it and ran back to the warm cab, and the big train rumbled on down the new track.

PROMISE ME SOMETHING

"Sure," Kate said. "Anything."

DON'T LET MY FIRE GO OUT

IT'S THE ONE THING I'M SCARED OF. I DON'T WANT TO GO TO THE ROUNDHOUSE!

Kate and Tom looked at each other.
"Sure. Of course."
"We promise," Tom said. "What's the Roundhouse?"

I CAN'T EVEN TALK ABOUT IT

After a few hours they entered a silent, misty forest. The tops of the trees disappeared overhead into thick fog. Kate knew it was still daytime, but the sun was hidden by the mist. It looked miles deep.

Still: so far so good. She found Tom in the dining car eating a muffin and looking out the window at the giant trees in the gloom.

"This is weird," he said.

"Eerie."

They didn't speak for a while. It was kind of hypnotic, staring into the misty depths.

"What kind of muffin is that?" she said.

"Banana chocolate."

"Are there any more?"

"There were two, but I ate them both."

She sighed. It was hard being philosophical about things all the time, but somehow she managed it.

Kate felt the train slow down and stop. Once again they weren't at a station—that was never a good sign. She went forward to talk to the *Silver Arrow*.

"Where are we?" Kate said.

I DON'T KNOW

"Oh." Kate considered that. "How about we keep going till we get to somewhere where we do know where we are?"

I DON'T THINK I CAN

I'M OUT OF COAL

Wait—really? Kate checked the tender again, and her insides went cold. Nothing but coal dust. A load was still burning in the firebox, but that would only last another few hours. Somehow she'd just assumed that they'd have enough to make it to the next station or fuel depot or whatever. These things always worked themselves out, right? Some part of her must still have thought, deep down, that somebody else would solve the problem.

But there was no one else, just her and Tom, and now they were stuck here alone in a strange forest who-knows-where, way off the main line, with no way to get home, and soon the *Silver Arrow*'s fire would go out. And that was its greatest fear.

Kate felt herself starting to panic. She wasn't even sure this problem had a solution. In video games, however bad things got, you knew there was always a way through to the next level. But real life wasn't like that. Sometimes there just was no way.

The trees outside were just ghostly shadows. Trees. Wait a second.

"I don't suppose," Kate said slowly, "that you could burn wood, could you? Instead of coal?"

The train hesitated.

IT'S NOT MY FAVORITE

"But if you really had to?"

I GUESS

IF I REALLY HAD TO

"Well, all right, then! We're in the middle of a forest! There's bound to be loads of branches and things. Everything here is fuel!"

Though when she climbed down from the train, Kate suddenly felt nervous and exposed. It was very still and quiet in the forest. There was no wind. No birds sang. It seemed like anything could come out of that mist at any moment.

But she couldn't think of any other plan. She wondered if this was what had happened to that other train, the one that never came back. Maybe they'd gotten stuck here, too, and been devoured by some hungry forest-dwelling mist monster. Something rustled behind her, and she spun around.

It wasn't a mist monster. It was the others: Tom, the heron, the fishing cat, the snake, even the porcupine.

"We thought you might want some company," the cat said.

"Especially since it's kind of spooky out here," the heron said.

"I just wanted a fresh gnawing stick," the porcupine said.

Kate smiled. Adventures were great, but she was learning that sometimes you didn't want to go on them alone.

Trees

SLOWLY AND CAUTIOUSLY THEY FANNED OUT into the forest. The train disappeared behind them in the fog almost immediately. It was ridiculously thick, as if there were a smoke machine somewhere nearby that was stuck on maximum.

The trees were absolutely enormous, and they had no branches low down, so they looked like big stone columns in a cathedral. The biggest ones were as thick around as an elephant. It was so quiet it was almost like they were holding themselves still.

There was only one problem: There wasn't any firewood. None. The forest floor was completely bare of branches.

"Where's all the sticks?" Tom said.

"I don't know."

It was as if somebody had come through right before them and tidied up. Kate looked up, but even the lowest branches were lost in the fog. There had to be a way. Without wood they'd be stranded here forever.

"Maybe we could chop one down," Tom said.

"Yeah. Except that we don't have an ax, and even if we did it would be completely impossible because they're like the size of buildings."

"True."

"Maybe the heron could fly up and get some branches." Though Kate knew the delicate heron could never get as many as they needed.

It almost felt like the forest was waiting for something from them. Kate guessed it made sense—here she was, just showing up like this, expecting to collect armloads of wood for free. Maybe it wanted something back.

That was fair. But what? What would a forest want?

"All right," she said quietly. "Hi, forest. We're looking for firewood to make our train go. Want to trade? What can we give you?"

The fishing cat cocked her head. "Who are you talking to?"

"Nobody!" Kate blushed. She didn't want to admit she was talking to a forest.

But she kept going in her head. *We really don't mind*, she thought. *We're happy to pay. We'd be grateful.*

And then it was the oddest thing, because a thought appeared in her head:

Are you sure?

It was a thought, but it wasn't her thought. It came in a voice that felt old, and very gentle, and very strong. And not alone, but like many voices speaking in unison.

It was the forest. She knew it.

I'm sure, she thought.

And that was that. It started as soon as she thought it.

The bottoms of her feet tingled. It wasn't unpleasant, but it gave her an uncontrollable urge to take off her shoes. And not just her shoes but her socks, too: Suddenly she was craving the feeling of prickly, loamy soil under her feet.

So she took them off. Tom was doing the same thing. The second her bare soles touched the ground, she curled her toes right into it. And the really weird thing was, her toes kept on going.

They were getting longer. They stretched and pushed down into the cold dirt, like when you bury your feet in the sand at the beach, but much, much more. She felt them going deeper and deeper into the dirt.

At the same time her legs were getting longer, and her arms. She was getting taller, growing so fast that the ground zoomed down away from her.

It should have been scary, but for some reason it just wasn't. It actually felt kind of amazing. Kate threw her suddenly huge arms wide, and as she did they stiffened, and her fingers spread and multiplied and then burst gloriously into twigs and foliage. She grew up, up, up, and it was like she was stretching her back after a long sleep. She was turning into a tree.

She closed her eyes. She didn't need them! There were so many other ways to sense and feel. Her toe-roots went down, down, down, winding and finding their way through layers

of delicious cold black earth as if it were mile-deep chocolate and at the same time spreading outward around her in a huge underground web, threading between pebbles and rocks and other roots, rubbing elbows with friendly worms, drinking in delicious chilled clear water that flowed funnily up through her legs and all through her body to feed her finger-branches and her leaf-hair.

The wind flowed past her, and she swayed with it like it was music. She grew so tall she could stick her crown up above the mist and feel the warmth of bright sunlight on it. It felt wonderful, like sunshine always does, except that now she was a tree, so she wasn't just feeling the sunlight, she was *eating* it. It was her food. And it tasted incredible.

And when it rained, she drank the rain, and that was delicious, too.

Her branches touched the tips of other trees' branches, and their roots mingled underground, as if they were holding hands but with their toes. The cat had become a pussy willow, and the heron was now a lovely gray ash tree. The mamba had become a magnificent African blackwood tree. The porcupine was a thorny honey locust.

They all stood together as a grove, and it was the calmest Kate had ever felt in her life. If she'd had to stand here like this as a girl she would've been bored silly, but as a tree she was never bored. She wasn't waiting for anything, or wishing she were somewhere else, she was just here, just now, all the time. Weeks went by while Earth spun like a carousel and the sun and moon and stars wheeled dizzily overhead.

Day and night changed places like a game. Birds weren't afraid of her, they loved her and nested in her branches. A friendly giant, she listened to the frisky low-level chatter of the little plants around her and the shadowy whispering of the fungi below that. It wasn't all fun; there were pain and strife, too. Insects and caterpillars fed on her. Birds pecked holes in her. Lightning licked down and scarred or demolished trees seemingly at random.

Autumn came and she let go of her

leaves—it was a relief, really, as though she'd been wearing a lovely ball gown that had gotten slightly uncomfortable and now she could finally take it off. When winter arrived she felt the cold but didn't mind it in the slightest, though sometimes the weight of ice made her ache. She dozed.

Then spring came, and she was washed by fresh rains and warmed by the new sun, and she came alert again. Her gorgeous leaves burst out like the feathers of a beautiful green bird. Years later, when she tasted champagne for the first time, she would remember being a tree in springtime and think: *Yes. This is like that.*

Summer was a grand feast of sunlight—but almost as soon as it started, something unexpected happened. She was...shrinking?

Her head dropped below the mist again, slipping down away from the sun. Her leaves and her branches—her magnificent, multitudinous branches—were withering, and her roots were letting go of the soil, pulling back up out of it like a ship weighing anchor, preparing to set sail again.

And then she opened her eyes, and there she was. That's right. She was Kate. She'd forgotten her name, but that was it: Kate. She was a girl. It was all coming back to her. Everything was so different: She was small and soft, and she wasn't rooted in the ground, she wandered around loose. She could see and talk and move, but she couldn't taste the soil or the sunlight anymore. What a weird way to live.

Everything looked the same as it had before. She was standing right in the same spot. The mist, the forest...did it all even happen? Was it all a dream?

But if it was a dream then the others had dreamed it, too. They were blinking and shuffling their feet. Kate felt lost and unsteady, being unplugged from the earth like that.

"We were trees," Tom said.

It was all anybody really needed to say. They walked a little shakily back toward where the train was still waiting. Next to it stood a great big pyramid of firewood, all neatly stacked.

And many old voices thought together in Kate's head:

Remember this.

He Thought He Could

THE *SILVER ARROW*'S FIRE WAS STILL GOING when they got back, though only barely. Kate and Tom fed logs into it till it was big and blazing again, and they set out along the branch line, running on wood now instead of coal.

Leaving the misty forest behind, they *clickety-clack*ed through miles of empty fields. Kate opened the doors and looked out at the grass skimming past. It was funny: From a moving train, things close to you slipped by so fast they were blurry, whereas the trees on the horizon looked like they were barely moving at all. Then the tracks merged with another set of tracks coming in from the right, so smoothly she didn't even feel a bump, and just like that they were back on course again, on the main line.

They got back to their regular routine, picking up animals and dropping them off, in lush rain forests, flaming autumn forests, frozen arctic forests of evergreens, dry thorny scrub forests, flooded swamp forests. Kate took ticket after ticket: AL-ANSARIYAH MOUNTAINS, MAOLAN KARST FOREST, CROTHERS WOODS, DYREHAVEN, FORÊT D'ÉPERLECQUES, LONE MOUNTAIN STATE FOREST. As quiet and dignified as they were when they got on, the animals were always excited to get where they were going—they scampered and loped and fluttered out through the doors the second they opened.

The *Silver Arrow* stopped for ibex and chinchillas. It picked up a massive bison who looked totally bizarre close up, like a bull from another planet, though he carried himself with great dignity. They picked up a pair of mighty-winged, bald-headed condors and a black-and-white-banded snake called a Malayan krait who was so venomous that she made even the mamba nervous. At one station a delicate, airy glass greenhouse car was added to the train, full of different-colored fluttery butterflies. They dropped it off again a few stops later.

Once they rumbled through a long tunnel under a mountain—miles long, it felt like. Kate worried for a second that the library car wouldn't fit, but it did. She switched on a light in the cab. (Interestingly—or Kate found it interesting—even though there were electric lights on the train, they actually ran off power from a little onboard electric generator that itself ran on steam power.) When they finally spotted a light at the end of the tunnel, it wasn't daylight, it was the yellow subterranean light of a subway station.

Men and women and girls and boys stood on the platform, all staring down at their phones. The train stopped and the doors opened. A single well-groomed owl stepped on.

Kate thought that people might potentially be interested in the fact that a huge steam train full of animals and driven by children had just come roaring into their subway station—but they never looked up from their phones. Not once. They never noticed. *It's like they're awake but they're asleep*, Kate thought. She swore silently to herself that she would try to never be that asleep herself.

Kate spent most of her time in between

stops in the library car, where she finished the book about the secret underground school-under-a-school and started a new one. They found a fuel depot and switched back over to coal. She explored deeper into the candy car, as far as the Swedish Fish section—she never knew they came in more than one flavor! When it was hot she swam in the swimming pool car, which was exactly as fun as you'd think swimming in a pool on a fast-moving train would be. Tom experimented to see whether he could walk all the way through both dining cars stepping only on tables and chairs. (He could.)

Kate took pride in keeping the brass fittings in the cab polished and the floor swept—she and Tom were always dropping bits of coal on their way from the tender to the firebox. When she'd first seen the cab it had looked like a mess of random pipes and levers to her, but now she could read the *Silver Arrow*'s controls like a book. She felt like she had a whole new set of senses: Some part of her mind was always keeping track of the water level and the steam pressure in the boiler, and the heat in the firebox, and how steep the grade was, and where the throttle and the reversing lever were set. (She totally got the reversing lever thing now.) Steam was old-fashioned technology, but it turned out that you could be a major nerd for it anyway.

They chugged uphill, switchbacking up into a steep mountainside forest. Gray slopes fell away behind them into green valleys, which wandered off and faded away into the distance. But as beautiful as it was, it was hard work climbing mountains. The *Silver Arrow* kept demanding more and more coal, and going slower, and slower, and slower, till after a while Kate could almost have kept up with it on foot.

She didn't want to think what would happen if they actually stopped, or even worse, started rolling back down the mountain. Tom kept whispering "I-think-I-can I-think-I-can" to the train, like in *The Little Engine That Could*, and the train kept telling him to knock it off.

I'M NOT DESIGNED TO CLIMB MOUNTAINS.
I'M NOT A FUNICULAR!

"I don't know what that is, but tell me if we have to start leaving cars behind," Kate said. "I can live without the boxcars, but I draw the line at the library car."

I'M NOT LOSING ANY CARS

WHAT KIND OF A MONSTER ARE YOU?

"I'm just trying to help."

WE LEAVE NO CAR BEHIND

EXCEPT MAYBE THE CANDY CAR, I'LL
LET YOU KNOW

Finally, they made it to the top, where there was a pass through the mountains. By this time the *Silver Arrow* was barely moving at a walking pace. The shadows of the mountains stretched away for miles behind them, spilling darkly down into the valley. For one long minute they were on level ground, and everybody sat back and took a deep breath.

Then the *Silver Arrow* tipped forward and started down the other side of the mountain.

It picked up speed quickly—and kept on picking it up. The chuffing and the *clickety-clack*ing accelerated, slowly at first, but then faster and faster. Kate stuck her head out the window, and the wind hit her in the face. Soon they were really moving, booming down the mountain, faster than they'd ever gone before. Kate and Tom exchanged a nervous look. It was a relief to be making good time again, but maybe this was too much of a good thing.

"I'm sorry I made fun of you for going slow before," Tom said. "If this is your revenge, you've made your point."

I'M NOT MAKING A POINT

I CAN'T SLOW DOWN

"Where's your speedometer?" Kate said.

DON'T HAVE ONE

"What?!"

STEAM ENGINES DON'T HAVE
SPEEDOMETERS

"Were you literally invented in medieval times? How're we supposed to know how fast we're going?!"

Kate could almost feel the weight of the heavy cars behind them, shoving them along. She shut off the steam and tried the brakes, first lightly and then harder.

OW! MY BRAKE SHOES!

It didn't work anyway. She barely felt the difference. It was official: The *Silver Arrow* had become a runaway train.

The cab started rocking scarily back and forth. They were cutting across a steep slope, and if they derailed that would be the end— they'd roll sideways, over and over, all the way down the mountain. The animals came crowding forward into the cab.

"We've come to express our concern," the cat said. "We're concerned that we're all going to die."

"I know!" Kate said. "I'm braking as hard as I can!"

"I almost fell on the porcupine," the snake said.

"The snake almost fell on me!" the porcupine said.

"I want you all to know," the heron said, "that if we fall off a cliff, I will survive by jumping out the window and flying away, but I'll remember you all fondly and in great detail."

"Thanks," Kate said without much enthusiasm.

"What's your brother's name again?"

"Tom!" said Tom.

"I'll never forget you, Tim."

"I can't believe birds used to be dinosaurs," Tom said.

When Kate put her head out the window again, she saw up ahead the worst thing she could possibly see: They were coming up on a tight curve on the edge of a sheer cliff, and they were going way too fast. Their momentum would take them right off it.

She threw herself on the brake lever and pushed.

IT'S ALREADY ALL THE WAY ON!

"If you can transform into an airplane or something, now would be a good time!"

THAT IS AN UNREASONABLE EXPECTATION!

It was too late anyway. The *Silver Arrow* hit the curve and Kate felt the whole train lean out to one side over thin air. Everybody screamed. Kate clung to the cab's left side, which was on the inside of the curve. Maybe her weight would make a tiny bit of difference?! She could actually feel the train's left-hand wheels leave the track, and for a horrible instant they were riding the curve on one single rail. There was the toe-curling shriek of steel on steel, and for an unbearably long second they balanced there and time seemed to stop—

—and then the train crashed back down onto the rails and they kept going.

The track was straight from there. They

rattled down the lower slopes of the mountain and on into the foothills. Kate looked around the cab.

"Let's never do that again," she said.

"Agreed," the heron said.

AGREED

As soon as she dared, Kate stuck her head back out the window to see what was coming next. She regretted it immediately.

"I don't believe it," she said.

They'd reached the coast, and up ahead were bright white sand and the wide blue ocean. The tracks led straight down into it.

The Wise Island

THIS TIME KATE DIDN'T BOTHER YELLING anything like "Look out!" or "Oh no!" or even just "Help!" It was already too late. All she could do was watch the wild blue surf come thundering up at them.

She closed her eyes. If she had to die at the age of eleven, she supposed that crashing into a nameless ocean in a speeding steam train with her brother and a bunch of talking animals at least had some flair to it. She would have an outstandingly compelling obituary.

But she didn't die. Instead the *Silver Arrow* swooshed right down into the water.

Kate wished she could've watched it from a distance because it would've looked so cool: The massive black steam engine charged right into the rolling surf, butting and smashing through the waves, throwing spray everywhere, seawater hissing off its hot boiler—and then the water parted and formed a luminous emerald tunnel down into the ocean, and the *Silver Arrow* shot right down into it.

Gradually, foot by foot, the tracks descended under the water, following the slope of the ocean floor. Shifting green sunlight filtered down through the ocean overhead, quickly cooling into a deep blue dusk as the tunnel took them farther below the surface. Sound became muffled. Rocks and seaweed and schools of silvery fish rolled past, eyeing them curiously and flashing their bright sides.

"Wow," Kate said. "Oh wow. What is even happening?"

DON'T ASK ME

BUT IT'S BEAUTIFUL

Kate reached out the window and let her fingertips skim along the side of the water-tunnel. A big blue blunt-headed fish a yard long floated past, nibbling at rocks, trailing a cloud of smaller fish that clung close to its sides. The *Silver Arrow* steamed along deeper and deeper under the sea till the water around them was almost black and the air got cold enough that Kate put on her heavy coat.

The last thing they saw before the light

faded completely was the enormous shadowy bulk of a sperm whale gliding slowly and majestically overhead like a blimp. Then the water was as black as night, broken only by the starry lights of a few phosphorescent fish.

At some point—Kate couldn't have said exactly when—the tracks ran down under the ocean floor itself, and the blackness became the blackness of an underground tunnel. She turned on the lights. The tunnel lasted for a good half hour before they came back up into dark water, then deep blue, then green, brighter and brighter till finally they burst out into a world of hot sunlight and white sand. It was so beautiful that Kate throttled down and hit the brakes even though they weren't at a station.

They were on a low sandy island in the middle of a glittering blue sea.

Most of Kate's experiences of beaches hadn't been at the ocean; they'd been at Lake Michigan, and they'd been a bit of a letdown. To save money, her family usually went in the off-season, when it wasn't really warm enough, and the beaches were narrow and gray and not very clean.

This was nothing like that. The sand here was fine and soft as flour and almost as white. It stretched up into a graceful, grassy-topped dune.

"This is practically my natural habitat!" the fishing cat said, and she bounded off into the water. The heron strode after her, and they proceeded to have a fishing contest, though it was hard to tell who won because they both kept eating their fish.

The mamba sunned himself in the sand.

"You warm-blooded creatures can have no idea what this feels like," he said. "Literally none. It's what ice must feel like when it's melting."

"I think I have some idea," Kate said. "I was a tree for while."

Kate and Tom took off their shoes and raced each other to the top of the dune, kicking up sprays of sand as they ran. From there they could see almost the whole island: an oval of white sand all by itself in the middle of an infinite ocean. We must be the only people around for hundreds of miles, Kate thought.

They fetched food from a dining car and borrowed a blanket from the sleeper car and had a picnic.

The porcupine sat on the blanket with them, contentedly gnawing a carrot. The baby pangolin bumbled around, playing games in the sand. He'd gotten much more active lately, sniffing and exploring everything with his startlingly long tongue. He had four legs but toddled around mostly on two, stooped over like a tiny scaly old man.

"I wonder how long this is going to last," Kate said.

"What, the picnic?"

"This whole thing. The train, the animals, the adventure. It feels like it's been weeks. I mean, I love it, but I miss Mom and Dad."

"Yeah, I do too," Tom said.

"I know we have to get the animals where they're going, but surely some of them could do it the old-fashioned way. You know. Like geese do."

Kate let her mind drift.

"I wonder if this island has a name," she said sleepily.

"Of course it does," said Tom. "It's the Wise Island."

"How could you possibly know that?"

"The train told me."

"Oh," Kate said. "What's so wise about it?"

"Well, you can dig for treasure."

Kate liked the sound of that. Though she still didn't see where wisdom came into it. And she was skeptical, as ever, about anything free.

"You can dig for treasure anywhere," she said. "Nobody ever finds any."

"That's the thing! You know how everybody always digs in the sand at the beach but

never finds anything? Here, if you dig, you find something!"

"What, automatically?"

He nodded. "Everybody finds one thing."

"Like gold and silver?"

"I don't know," Tom said. "I don't think it's that kind of treasure. But the train said it's different for everybody."

They didn't dig right away. First they walked up and down the beach a couple of

times, surveying the area, sometimes skipping away from the waves that slid up the sand, sometimes letting them wash over their bare feet. They found some shells, beautiful candy-striped pink-and-white cones. The water was warm and as clear as glass—you could see fish darting around in it, just out of reach.

Kate and Tom debated where they should dig. They weren't sure whether the location mattered, if you automatically found something anyway, but you never knew. Kate wondered what kind of treasure could possibly be there in the absolute middle of nowhere. Eventually Tom chose a spot well up the beach, above the tidemarks, near where the dunes started. Kate ended up walking all the way back to where they'd first sat down, where the mamba was still sunning himself blissfully in the powdery sand. She plopped down on the picnic blanket and started scooping out a hole with her hands right next to it.

She quickly got down past the sun-warmed upper layer and into the cold, coarse, wet sand underneath. She dug farther and farther, as deep as her elbows and then even farther, till she'd reached the water level and her fingers were getting raw and she had to lean her whole arm down into the hole up to her shoulder.

She wondered if Tom could've been pranking her—but no, he was still digging away at his own hole. Maybe the island had decided she wasn't worthy.

Just then her fingers brushed something hard and smooth.

It was so far down she could barely scrabble at it with her fingertips, but she stretched and stretched, and finally she managed to hook her fingers under it. It was stuck fast in the sand, but she tugged and heaved at it till it finally pulled free.

It was a small, flat metal box, closed tight with a clasp. Kate wondered what kind of treasure could possibly come in a box that small. She undid the latch and opened it. Inside the box was a little case, and inside the case, which was lined with deep blue velvet, was a pair of tortoise-shell glasses.

There was a neat handwritten tag tied to the glasses with string. It said:

*These are the glasses
that Grace Hopper wore
when she first learned to
program a computer*

They just looked like ordinary glasses—but to Kate they were more precious than a diamond-studded tiara. *Grace Hopper's eyes looked through these same lenses*, she thought. Through these frames Grace Hopper read the things that her furiously smart brain told her furiously smart fingers to type. Things that had changed history.

And they were kind of cool-looking, too, in a retro-vintage way.

Kate carefully placed the glasses back in their case and closed it. She would keep them forever. Her vision was perfect, but she decided that as soon as possible she would ruin it by reading too much and writing too much brilliant code, and then she would wear these glasses for the rest of her life.

She was about to show Tom what she'd found—but he'd found something, too. He was holding a small, tattered stuffed fox, orange with a brown tail. He was hugging it with tears running down his face.

Kate knew that fox. His name was Foxy, full name Foxy Jones. He was the one that Tom had lost on that skiing trip all those years ago—the one he'd had since he was a baby, the one he'd thought he'd lost forever. And now Foxy Jones was back for good.

The *Twilight Star*

THEN ONE DAY, AS THE TRAIN WAS PUFFING across a plain of scrub so flat that it looked like somebody had made it with a ruler, and the little pangolin had graduated to eating bits of raw hamburger from the dining car—which they were all very proud of him for—Kate strolled back through the passenger cars and noticed they were looking emptier than usual. Fewer animals were getting on, and more were getting off.

A few days after that they were down to just the animals from the library: the fishing cat, the white-bellied heron, the green mamba, and the porcupine.

Plus the sleeping polar bear. And the baby pangolin. That was when they started what was in some ways the hardest part of the whole trip.

They crossed into a frozen desert, mile after mile of empty sand dunes covered in thin tiger stripes of frost and snow. They steamed across it for days. Dry powdery snow and sand whispered and rattled against the windowpanes when the wind blew. The porcupine was grumpier than usual and complained that he wasn't getting his fair share of time with the pangolin. Once they came to a tunnel with a sign outside that said DANGER! FALLING ROCKS! and Kate and Tom had to get a squeaky old handcar out of one of the boxcars and pump it along ahead of the train all the way through the tunnel, in the freezing cold, to make sure the tracks were clear.

Another time the *Silver Arrow* almost ran out of water, till Tom remembered that they had a whole swimming pool car full of it.

At night either Kate or Tom would sit up with the *Silver Arrow* while the other one slept curled up in their cozy bunk in the sleeper car. They kept an eye out for dangerous curves and warning signals and steep slopes and anything that might be blocking the tracks. More than once they had to stop and shovel away drifts of windblown sand.

It went on for so long that Kate started to wonder how much more she could take. There were dark shadows under her eyes, and when she closed them, all she saw was more track scrolling past her. She was so tired she kept bumping into hot brass pipes in the cab and burning herself. At the same time the bitter chill of the desert spread deeper into the train, so they could see their breath inside, and even when Kate huddled right up next to the fire-box she still couldn't seem to get warm.

Where am I? Kate thought. *What am I doing out here?* It felt like she'd been on the *Silver Arrow* forever. It was the adventure of a lifetime, but it was a whole lot of work, too. And it was taking a really long time.

Then one morning, very early, in the still, frozen hour right before dawn, the train slowed down again. She looked out the window, but they weren't at a station.

Click-*bing.*

LOOK UP AHEAD

Kate yawned, stretched, and stuck her head out the window. She saw what it meant.

"What the heck is that?"

I WOULD ALSO LIKE TO KNOW WHAT THE HECK THAT IS

It was hard to be sure, but up ahead in the darkness it looked like the land dropped away in a sheer cliff. But the tracks didn't stop at the cliff. They kept on going, right out over the cliff, into thin air.

Kate got out of the train and walked ahead, in the glow of the *Silver Arrow*'s headlight. At first the tracks kept going straight, but as her eyes got more used to the darkness Kate saw that farther on they curved upward like roller-coaster tracks, steeper and steeper, until they ran straight up into the dark, cloudy sky.

Kate chewed her lip, thinking. She walked back to the train.

"How are we going to get up that?" she said. "You can't go up that, can you?"

NO

Kate thought for a while.
"Is there another way round?" Kate said.

I DON'T THINK SO

"Can you go backward?"

YES

The train followed up this admirably brief
answer with a not-at-all-brief lecture
about the wonders of the reverser
and something called the
Walschaerts valve gear,
which was invented
by the heroic
but unsung
Belgian

engineer Egide Walschaerts (1820–1901) and which made it easier for steam locomotives to go in reverse. But I'm going to leave that part out. You're welcome.

"Then maybe we should go back," Kate said.

MAYBE WE SHOULD

Kate didn't say anything. She pressed her icy hands against her face. She was so tired and so cold. All she could think about was running into her house and diving into her warm, old bed and sleeping for a week. But that would mean abandoning her job, which was to get these animals to where they were going. And they weren't just animals, they were her friends.

But what else could she do? It was impossible. It was out of her hands. The idea of quitting made her sad, but it also—she hated to admit it—filled her with infinite relief. Maybe this job was just too big for her. She was only eleven, after all.

"I don't want to give up," she said. But her voice sounded hollow. She really, really wanted to give up.

NO ONE WOULD BLAME YOU

"Could I still keep the glasses?" Her voice was very small. "Grace Hopper's glasses? Even if we don't really finish the job?"

YOU COULD EVEN KEEP THE GLASSES

But they wouldn't have finished. That bothered Kate. It felt like the kind of thing the old Kate would've done, the person she was back before all this started. Being on the train had taught her to take responsibility for things, not just play things but real things. But some things were simply impossible. That was reality, too.

WHY DON'T YOU TAKE A WALK

"How's that going to help?"

DON'T ASK ME, I DON'T EVEN HAVE LEGS

BUT HUMANS ALWAYS SEEM TO DO IT
WHEN THEY NEED INSPIRATION

So she took a walk. If nothing else it might warm her up.

She didn't leave the train. Instead she did something that everybody always wants to do but hardly anybody ever gets to, which is to walk along the roof of a train. Whenever you take a train you can clearly see there are ladders to get up there, but for some ridiculous reason nobody's ever allowed to use them except train conductors and people having fistfights in action movies.

Now was her chance. She climbed up a ladder onto the roof of a passenger car and set off. It wasn't even hard: The roof was about ten feet wide, though it did curve slightly upward in the middle, and there was a gap between the cars that was just wide enough to make her heart flutter a little. She wondered if she could do this when the train was moving. How cool would that be?

But she was just distracting herself. That was something the animals never did, she realized. People looked down on animals, but animals never made excuses or felt sorry for themselves. It would never occur to them. They always looked problems in the face.

Kate walked all the way back to the caboose, which she'd never even visited before. It was painted red, and there was a small stove inside, and bunks, and a desk. It was like a clubhouse. At the very back there was a balcony where you could sit and watch the track reel out behind you. She made a mental note to come back here later. Though then she remembered there probably wouldn't be a later.

It was when she was walking back that Kate noticed a very old set of rusty-brown train tracks leading off through the grass and into a grove of trees. They were as old and rusty as the ones behind her house used to be. She climbed down and followed them.

It was still bitter cold, but at least the sun was rising now. She stepped from one thick old wooden tie to the next till she reached the trees.

She didn't exactly find inspiration there. But she did find another steam engine.

It was just standing there on a siding, which Kate now knew was a piece of track where you stored trains that nobody was using. Nobody had used this steam train for a long time.

Its paint was gone, and rust had turned the train completely brick red. In places it had eaten right through the metal, and you could see into the darkness of the big boiler, where the steam used to be. All the glass in the windows was gone. Grass and weeds had grown up through the spokes of the rusty wheels, which would never turn again.

Once it must have been as fast and proud and

powerful as the *Silver Arrow*. It had thundered down tracks snorting steam and hauling long strings of cars. But those days were gone. You could never fix this train, it was way past that.

But you could still make out its name in very, very faint faded paint:

THE TWILIGHT STAR

Kate reached out and touched the brittle, flaking metal.

"I'm sorry, *Twilight Star*," she said. "I bet you were a great train."

This was it, this was what Uncle Herbert had asked them to look out for. Well, she'd found it. It wasn't a real star, it was a train. She wondered who'd left it there. Did they know it was forever when they left? Did they tell it they'd come back but then never did? A robin flitted out through the train's window and off into the brightening air. It must have a nest in there, Kate thought. So at least it had the birds to keep it company.

Kate walked back to the *Silver Arrow* with her head full of thoughts.

"I found something," Kate said. "An old train called the *Twilight Star*."

OH

"Have you heard of it?"

**THAT WAS THE NAME OF THE TRAIN
BEFORE ME**

THE ONE THAT DIDN'T COME BACK

So that's what had happened to it.
"This must have been as far as it got."

IT MUST HAVE BROKEN DOWN HERE

AND ITS CONDUCTORS MUST HAVE GIVEN
UP AND GONE HOME

"Oh. But then what would've happened to them?"

NOTHING

THAT WAS THE END OF THEIR
ADVENTURE

"What about the animals?"

I GUESS THEY HAD TO FEND FOR
THEMSELVES

IT WOULDN'T HAVE BEEN EASY. BUT
THEY'RE USED TO IT

Kate didn't say anything more for a while. She sat and looked around at the *Silver Arrow*'s cab, which had seemed so weird when she'd first seen it and which now felt so much like home. She imagined it old and rusty and ruined like the *Twilight Star*. Sitting all by itself in the wind and rain and snow, alone and abandoned.

"I would never leave you here," she said quietly. But the *Silver Arrow* didn't answer. Maybe it didn't believe her. Maybe it was right.

She couldn't go back, but she didn't know how to go forward, either. She knew it was wrong to give up, but when people said you should never give up, they never talked about how hard it was to keep going! Maybe part of being an adventurer was knowing when the adventure was over. Maybe that was another one of those life lessons she was supposed to be learning.

But then she thought about the animals. And the *Silver Arrow*. She closed her eyes, and a tear squeezed out. She wiped it away and walked back to the library car.

Chins

THE HERON HAD FOUND AN OLD BOOK FULL of paintings of birds and was leafing through it, turning the pages with the tip of her long beak. The fishing cat had gone for a chilly swim in the swimming pool car and was drying her fur by the woodstove, fast asleep. The mamba was hanging from the overhead lamp, looking like a piece of loose green electrical cable. Kate could never figure out how he got up there.

The baby pangolin was curled into a ball, which the porcupine rolled back and

forth along the carpeted floor. The pangolin seemed to enjoy this.

"So," Kate said. "There's a problem."

"What kind of problem?" the heron said.

Kate explained. The animals all thought for a minute.

"If quills would help with this situation in any way," the porcupine said, "just say the word."

"Thank you." Though Kate was pretty sure it wasn't that kind of problem.

There was another long silence, in the middle of which the fishing cat woke up and asked what was going on and Kate had to explain everything all over again.

The heron closed her big book.

"Do you remember," she said, "when we talked about invader species and why they're bad?"

"Yes."

"There was one invasive species we didn't mention. An especially bad one, a kind of ape. They have weirdly enlarged heads and hardly any fur."

"Oh, they're the worst," the porcupine said.

"I think I see where you're going with this," Kate said.

"Also they have chins," said the cat. "It's the strangest thing: a bony spur right under the lower jaw. No other animal on the planet has them."

"Okay," Kate said. "Okay. I get it."

"They're not just an invasive species; they're the original invasive species that created all the other ones. We get mad at starlings, but if you think about it, it's not really their fault. They never asked to be released in North America. They don't care about Shakespeare. Without those hairless chinny apes, there might not be any invasive species at all.

"And that's just the beginning. They create all kinds of other problems, too. Building everywhere, cutting down trees, damming rivers, changing the atmosphere, heating up the oceans—I mean, forget about squirrels; those apes are making a dozen species extinct *every single day*. They're making pangolins extinct by catching them and grinding them up into medicine. And the medicine doesn't even work!"

"I get it." Kate sat down in an armchair glumly. "You're talking about humans."

"What I still don't understand," the porcupine said, "is how you did it all without quills."

"Or venom," said the snake.

"Or wings."

"You know what I could go for right now?" the cat said. "A nice fish."

"You asked before where we were all going," the heron said, "and I think nobody wanted to say it, but the truth is that we're running away from you."

Kate looked around at the animals. She'd become so fond of them.

"I didn't realize," she said in a small voice.

"Green mambas aren't endangered," the snake said. "I'd like to see you humans endanger a mamba! But you're tearing down my forest, so I'm going to Mozambique. The fishing cats are in real trouble, though."

"It's true." The cat began washing her

face as casually as if she were talking about the weather. "There aren't many of us left. People hunt us and trap us and poison us. They're paving over our lovely marshes. I'm here because they're draining my mangrove swamp to build a hotel. But the white-bellied herons are even worse off."

"Oh, nonsense," the heron said modestly.

"Go on! You must be down to a few hundred."

The great bird sighed. "It's true. At this point we're almost extinct. People hunt us and steal our eggs. They dammed my river to make a power plant."

For a moment nobody spoke.

"We're fine," the porcupine said. "Thanks for asking, everybody. No shortage of porcupines."

"Everything's changing," the heron said. "Animals are on the move all over the world. We're refugees, just like people. Look at the poor polar bear!"

"What about her?" Kate said miserably.

"She was waiting for the train," the mamba

said, "but her station was made of ice. It melted in the warm weather and she was left swimming by herself in the middle of the ocean. By the time you came, it was almost too late."

Kate had slumped all the way down in her armchair. She felt like she was going to melt, too, into a puddle of shame. In that moment she wished she could un-hear everything the animals had just told her. She wished she'd stayed home and never gotten on the *Silver Arrow*. She'd thought she was escaping from her boring pointless life, but this was so much worse, and the worst part of all was that it was all her fault. When you're a child the adult world looks so exciting, and it is, but it's also so much sadder and more complicated than you expect. And you can't just take the good parts, you have to take it all, even if it's not what you wanted.

And once you do, there's no going back.

"You must hate us," she whispered. "You must hate us so much."

"But we don't," the heron said. "Not really."

And that was the strangest part: It was true. There was no hate in their voices.

"Hate is a human thing," the fishing cat said.

"We can do anger," the porcupine said. "Personally, I do it a lot. But not hate."

"So you can see why we're not that worried about the problem with the train," the heron said.

"You mean—because we're all going to die anyway?" Kate said.

"No. We're not worried because there is nothing more terrifyingly effective and resourceful than a human being. In all the four billion years that there has been life on Earth, you are the most successful animal there ever was. You're better than us at everything. If you want to fix this problem, you will, because when human beings want something, nothing gets in their way."

"But we're awful!" Kate moaned. "We've done such terrible, terrible things!"

"Yes," the heron said. "You absolutely have. But as animals go, you exhibit an unusually wide variety of behaviors. Some humans are terrible, but others aren't bad at all. Some are almost good."

"A good human being," the fishing cat said. "Imagine what one of those could do."

"They could do anything," the snake said quietly. "Anything at all."

Kate raised her head. They were all looking at her: the snake with his black lidless eyes, the cat with her green ones. The porcupine's eyes were jet beads. The heron's were a striking burnt orange, and perfectly circular.

After everything humans had done to

them, they still had hope. Whatever happened, the animals would never, ever give up. They couldn't. They didn't have that luxury. When Kate saw that, she knew that she couldn't either. Grace Hopper used to have a clock on her wall that ran backward, to show that you could always do things differently, no matter what. Kate would be a different kind of human.

She wasn't going home. She was going to get these animals where they needed to go. Back before the *Silver Arrow*, which seemed like a really long time ago now, she used to wish that life was like it was in books, that the whole world was in danger and it was up to her to save it.

She understood now that it was all true. The world really was in danger, and it really was up to her.

She stood up.

"I'll see what I can do," Kate said.

What Kate Could Do

"I HAVE NO IDEA WHAT TO DO," KATE SAID. "literally none."

She was back in the cab with Tom. She'd felt good for a minute there, like she really was the hero of one of those stories, but now that feeling was gone. Her mind was a complete blank.

Tom was watching her.

"What?"

"Why don't you ask me?" he said.

"Ask you what?"

"If I have any ideas."

She had to admit it hadn't occurred to her.

"To be honest, Tom," Kate said, "I go to you when I need something either eaten or broken. I think of myself as the planning department around here."

"Seems like you're all out of plans, though."

Kate opened her mouth to answer, but before she could, there was a click-*bing* from the *Silver Arrow*.

YOU KNOW, KATE

Hm. The train didn't usually use Kate's actual name.

"What?"

I JUST WANTED TO SAY

THAT THIS MIGHT BE ONE OF THOSE MOMENTS IN LIFE

THAT DOESN'T CALL FOR A SMART REMARK

Tom said nothing, just folded his arms and waited. Kate rolled her eyes.

Though it was true, she had spent a lot of time lately learning about animals and trains, and she hadn't been paying much attention to her brother. And Tom had come all this way with her. He'd worked just as hard. He hadn't quit either. He deserved to be listened to.

"Okay. Do you really have an idea?"

"Yes."

"Is it like that idea you had that one time about jumping off the garage roof using a trash bag from the kitchen as a parachute? And you broke your collarbone?"

"This one," Tom said, "is even better than that."

Kate made a hurry-it-up gesture.

"First say I'm awesome and you're glad I came on the trip with you."

OMG. Doing the right thing could be downright unpleasant sometimes.

"Fine. You're awesome and I'm glad you came on the trip with me."

"Okay," Tom said. "So while you've been

hanging out with the animals in the library, I've been exploring the train."

"Great. How does that help?"

"Because," Tom said, "it means that I've looked inside the mystery car, and you haven't."

Kate had completely forgotten it was there.

She'd seen it from the outside, of course. It wasn't especially mysterious-looking. In fact, it looked exactly like an ordinary old-fashioned boxcar: wooden, not steel, and painted a pale, watery blue. But it had a small door on one side, and now that she looked closely, she saw that it had something painted on it, in faded white paint:

?

Tom waited outside while Kate opened the door and looked.

"Right?" Tom said.

Kate nodded. All that extra energy of his did come in handy sometimes.

"When you're right," she said, "you're right."

"We should probably talk about this with the *Silver Arrow*."

"Maybe. Maybe not, though. It's disappointingly sensible about things like this."

They went back up to the engine together.

WELL?

"We're backing up." Tom put the engine in reverse.

WHY?

ARE WE GIVING UP?

"We're not giving up," Kate said. "We're backing up."

HOW FAR?

"Just enough," Tom said. "Let's say a mile."

"Enough for what?"

"Enough," Kate said. "Do you trust us?"

There was a pause from the *Silver Arrow*. A long one. Finally it typed:

yes

"Wow," Tom said. "I didn't know you even had a font that small."

MAYBE WE SHOULD PUT KATE BACK IN CHARGE THOUGH

"No, this is good," Kate said. "You were right. Tom knew what to do."

AND I'M ALL FOR ENCOURAGING HIM BUT

"Good."

After they'd backed up about a mile, Tom brought them to a stop. He gave the engine some steam, and the *Silver Arrow* started moving forward again. Faster. And faster. Soon they were really moving.

Tom hit the whistle:

FOOOOM! FOOOOOOOOOM!

The *chuff-chuff* of the engine was in double time and getting even faster, merging into a continuous roar. Kate looked outside. There was no stopping now, even if they wanted to.

"Go, Kate!" Tom shouted.

Kate sprinted back through the train to the mystery car.

"Find something to hang on to!" she called to the animals as she shot through the library.

What she'd seen inside the mystery car were two enormous metal cylinders bolted onto the arms of a massive steel girder shaped like a *T*. The cylinders were bright unpainted steel and flared out into huge cones pointing backward. It was pretty much impossible to mistake them for anything other than what they were: a pair of rocket engines.

"I knew Uncle Herbert should've gotten us a rocket!" Kate said to herself.

Unsurprisingly, the operation of rocket engines wasn't something that the *Silver Arrow* had covered in their training sessions.

Fortunately, these particular rocket engines didn't seem too complicated. In between them on the *T*-shaped support was a single small red button. A label under the button read: PUSH ME THEN RUN AWAY

Kate pushed the button.

Immediately, powerful pneumatic mechanisms roared to life and shoved the cylinders outward in both directions, right out through the wooden sides of the boxcar, with a shuddering *crash*. Splinters flew everywhere. The rocket engines were now sticking out on either side of the train.

Kate ran away as fast as she could.

A calm voice began to count down from ten. Kate thought maybe it should've picked a higher number to count from, and if she ever had the chance, she would report that as a design flaw. She made it through the boxcars, through the candy car, across the flat car, and all the way to the library car before the rockets kicked in.

Kicked was the right word: It felt like a giant soccer player had reared back and booted the train right in the caboose. Or like it really was a silver arrow and it was being fired from a huge bow. Kate flew right off her feet and slammed into the back wall of the library.

She stuck there like Velcro: The train was accelerating so fast it pinned her against the wall. Everything else in the room that wasn't nailed down joined them on the back wall. (Fortunately somebody had thought to nail down the furniture. Though not any of the cushions.) Fighting the g-forces, Kate could just turn her head far enough to see the world outside racing past in the window, faster and faster, even faster than they'd gone down the mountain. The whole train was shuddering and rocking with the force of the acceleration. She couldn't see them, but the rockets were now shooting out bright blue-white spikes of flame behind them, shoving the train forward faster and faster and faster toward the edge of the cliff.

The pressing question in Kate's mind was, did the rockets have enough power to push an entire steam train straight up a more-or-less vertical track? And if they did have enough power, where was that track going to take them?

The fields outside disappeared: The *Silver Arrow* had cleared the cliff. Now there was nothing but empty blue sky in the windows, and the train was still accelerating. Then it started tilting back, back and back and back as the track under it bent up toward the sky, back and farther back till every nerve in Kate's body was screaming, *Stop! Stop! For the love of all that is good and reasonable, stop!*

But rockets don't come with brakes. These didn't even have an OFF button. One of the wooden bars gave way, and Kate was pelted with a shelf's worth of books. They kept going up and up, blasting up through the clouds, and then Kate could feel something even crazier happening: The track kept curving back past the vertical, back in the direction of upside-down—but the rockets were driving

them so hard that centrifugal force kept them stuck to the track. The track kept curving till it did a complete roller-coaster loop, and for one delirious, transcendent moment they were completely upside down, with Kate's head pointed at the earth, and she went weightless, and in that moment all her fear suddenly evaporated into nothing and she laughed out loud with the awesomeness of it all.

And then they were past it and roaring down the downslope, still at high speed but no longer accelerating. Kate and the books and everything else slid down the wall and back to the floor, where they belonged.

Her whole body felt limp and spent. The noise of the rocket engines faded and then stopped. She managed to get on her feet and stagger to the window. Outside, underneath them, there were only clouds.

They were on a railroad in the sky.

"Is everybody okay?" she whispered.

Click-*bing*.

OMG THAT WAS AMAZING

The Train Station
in the Sky

THE *SILVER ARROW* WAS ROLLING ALONG ON
top of a cloud.

Click-*bing*.

**IF THIS IS DEATH, IT REALLY ISN'T THAT
BAD**

It was a long way down. Ahead and behind,
train tracks curved off through the sky into
the distance, looking very thin and precarious.

Kate made her way forward, wondering
what was up here in the clouds that could

be worth all that. She found herself stepping lightly and carefully, as if she might somehow fall out of the train at any moment.

But now she could see a station ahead of them. It looked like an ordinary country train station—a long, narrow platform with a railing and a little shelter—except that it was floating a mile in the air, and it was completely made of clouds. It was like somebody had decided to build an entire station out of fluffy white cotton wool.

She found the animals in the dining car.

"I wonder whose stop this is," Kate said.

"Not my natural habitat," the porcupine said.

"It's not even mine," the heron said.

"I think I might know," the fishing cat said.

She looked over at the baby pangolin, who had survived the rocket ride unscathed and apparently fast asleep, curled up safely in a scaly little ball.

"The pangolin's?" Kate said. "Pangolini? Whatever? I don't understand. Where are we?"

"I don't know," the snake said. "But it's somewhere very magic."

Kate picked up the pangolin, and he opened his wise, dark eyes and looked up at her. He'd definitely grown since that first day when she'd mistaken him for a pine cone, but he still weighed hardly anything. She carried him forward to the passenger car and opened the door.

She felt around with her foot, the way you would with thin ice, but the cloud platform was perfectly solid. Very carefully, she stepped out onto it. It was soft but bouncy, like a firmly stuffed cushion. It would've been fun to jump around on it, but for some reason

Kate wasn't in a jumping mood. This was a strangely solemn place.

Tom climbed down after her, followed by the other animals. There was nobody here to meet them. A cool wind blew. It gave Kate a floaty, dizzy feeling to be up this high.

This couldn't be right. Were they supposed to just leave the little pangolin up here in the middle of the sky all by himself? Alone, like she'd found him? She sat down cross-legged on the platform, in the shadow of the huge train, with the pangolin in her lap. The others stood around her.

Usually there was a sign telling you where the station was, but the sign here just read SOMEDAY.

"What does that mean?" she said. "*Someday*? That's not a place."

"It means there is no place for him," the fishing cat said. "Not now. Not yet. There's nowhere in the world we can take him that's safe enough. He'll just have to stay up here till things get better."

Kate looked down at the pangolin in her

lap, with his silly, lost little pine-cone face, and a tear fell onto one of his brown scales. He licked Kate's nose with his weirdly long pink tongue. It seemed incredible to Kate that anybody would ever do anything to hurt him. She wanted to hold him and keep him safe forever.

But it wasn't that people wanted to hurt him, she thought. Not really. They just weren't paying attention to him. They didn't care.

They weren't thinking about baby pangolins, they were just thinking about themselves.

But you have to think about them. You can't forget them. Kate resolved that always, wherever she was, whatever she was doing, she would remember baby pangolins. She saw now what she was supposed to do. She gave the pangolin a kiss and placed him all by himself on the platform.

"Goodbye," she said. "I love you."

The baby pangolin gave her a last look, sniffed, then unrolled and began bumbling around happily, just the way he always did.

Kate stepped back into the passenger car, where the others were already waiting, and even as she did, the cloud station began to change shape. It was softening and melting, turning itself into a soft little island for the pangolin. It would keep him safe till there was somewhere real for him to go.

The train gave a mighty hiss and puff and pulled away from the station in the sky.

Some problems in this world just don't have answers. Not yet.

Never, Ever

KATE KNEW WHAT WAS COMING NEXT, BUT she wasn't sure she was ready for it.

They rode through the sky all day. As the sun set, the track gradually bent down toward the earth until sometime in the night it touched down on a mountain peak. The *Silver Arrow* was hurrying now—it kept fretting that it was late in the season to be on this route. They didn't stop till the morning, when they reached a small, neat station with a corrugated-tin roof and vines hanging down all around it. The air was humid and smelled like exotic flowers and growing things. The heat hadn't come up yet, but you could tell it was going to be a hot day.

Kate stood in front of the open door. A voice spoke close beside her.

"This is me," the mamba said.

"It is? Where are we?"

"Mozambique. This is the East African coastal forest. Lots of mambas here."

Kate squatted down to meet the snake's dark, unblinking eyes. She remembered how frightened of him she'd been when they'd first met. Now when he reared up and slid himself around her neck, she didn't mind at all.

In fact, the cool, dry smoothness of the mamba felt lovely on her skin. He was as long as she was tall, but so slender that he barely weighed anything.

"We mambas are really very shy, you know," he said. "But I don't feel shy with you."

"I don't feel shy with you, either."

"Thank you for getting me here, Kate. I know it wasn't easy."

"It was an honor. It was the least I could do. I mean after . . . you know. Everything else."

"Don't feel too bad about what humans have done," the mamba said with a gentleness in his voice that she'd never quite heard before. "Feeling guilty doesn't help anything anyway. Humans are animals doing what all animals do: surviving. It's just that you've done it too well, so well that now you have to become a new kind of animal, one who makes sure that all the others survive, too."

The mamba slid noiselessly out the door and across the platform, a vivid green squiggle, and vanished into the forest.

The next stop was by a wide, shallow, milky-pale river that ran fast over rocks.

"My turn," the white-bellied heron said.

She stepped out onto the platform on her twiggy legs. They still looked weird to Kate, even if her knees really did bend forward.

"I don't suppose you come to Bhutan very often," the heron said.

"Not really." Kate hadn't actually been aware until that moment that Bhutan was a country.

"Not a lot of people do."

"I guess that makes it a good place to be a heron," Kate said.

"Exactly."

"I'll try my best to keep humans from destroying everything. I really will."

The heron nodded her beautiful crested head.

"I know." She brushed Kate's hand with her wing. "It may be too late for us. The last white-bellied heron will probably die in your lifetime. We were beautiful, and we hurt no one, but that wasn't enough.

"Just promise me you won't give up. The world has lost its old balance, but it's not too late. It could still find a new one."

She spread her wide wings and flapped away, gliding to land on an old log in the river, where she began searching the water for fish.

When the heron was gone, Kate walked

back to the library car. Only the fishing cat and the porcupine were left. Even after Tom came in to join them, it felt very empty.

Kate sat down on the couch, and for the first time ever the fishing cat came and sat in her lap. She was so big that she overflowed Kate's legs on either side like a big dog.

"Would you mind terribly much," the cat said, "scritching me behind my ears?"

"I was just going to ask if you'd *mind* if I scritched behind your ears."

Kate scratched gently.

"Mmmmmm. That's good. I can do it myself with my hind leg, but it's so much better with fingers."

She started to purr—a deeper, louder, more rumbling purr than a house cat's. Kate had never heard her purr before.

"I didn't know you could do that," Kate said.

"There are two kinds of cats in the world: roaring cats and purring cats. You can't do both. Lions roar. Tigers roar. But fishing cats are purring cats."

Kate was glad fishing cats could purr.

All too soon the train slowed down again. Kate had known these animals for only a few weeks, but somehow she felt closer to them than she did to anyone in the world except her family. Now she'd probably never see them again. Kate bent down and smooshed her face into the fishing cat's furry neck, and a couple of tears leaked out.

But it was so amazing that she'd gotten to meet them at all. She would always have that. When it was time, the fishing cat jumped lightly down from her lap, and together they walked forward to the passenger cars.

The train pulled in at a station in a huge marsh full of curious-looking trees that stood up above the water on long, stiff roots like stilts. There were so many of them so close together that they were all woven into one another. The air smelled like the ocean.

The station itself was all made of tropical wood, with a hairy-looking thatched roof.

"Where are we?" she said.

"We're in a mangrove forest," the fishing cat said.

"How can trees grow like this? In the sea, I mean."

"Mangroves grow in salt water," the cat said. "They're the only trees in the world that can."

It started to rain, a light, warm rain, but that didn't seem to bother the fishing cat.

"I'll probably never see you again," Kate said.

"I know."

"It makes me so sad, it feels like I can't stand it! Don't animals get sad?"

"Of course we do," the fishing cat said. "But we try not to brood about it. Animals never think about what might have been, or what should have been. We only ever think about what really is."

"I'll try to remember that." Kate leaned down and gave the cat a kiss on the top of her head. "And I'll always remember you."

"I'll remember you, too, Kate. And I want to tell you something, just to make sure you know it, just in case your parents are too busy to remind you as often as they should: You are special, Kate. You are strong and smart and good, and the world needs you."

Kate's eyes were blurry and swimming with tears. It was the one thing she'd always wanted to hear, all her life. If anybody else had said it, she might have had trouble believing it, but she knew she could trust the fishing cat.

"Thank you," she said.

"You're welcome. Ooh—a frog!"

And with that the cat took a running leap into the water and disappeared.

After that, whenever Kate was feeling down— which would always happen, because you're never too grown up to feel down sometimes— she would think about the fact that somewhere out there in the world, in a mangrove swamp, was a fishing cat who remembered her.

And that was something. It was a lot, really.

In all the excitement Kate had almost forgotten about the polar bear, but of course she was still with them, in her boxcar. They let her off late that night at a station deep in the Arctic, right out onto the pack ice. It was the coldest air Kate had ever felt. The wind whipped snow in through the open doors so hard that she had to scrunch her face up and look away. Before she did, she caught a glimpse of a sign that said simply NORTH POLE.

The polar bear paused on her way out into the blizzard. Kate had never heard her speak before, but now she put her great black muzzle right up to Kate's ear and said the first and last words that Kate would ever hear her say. Her voice was deep and rumbly.

"If you humans let us die, you will never, ever forgive yourselves."

The Journey Home

KATE AND TOM AND THE PORCUPINE HUDDLED together around the firebox in the cab.

"Right," Kate said, raising her voice over the *clackety-clack* of the train. "Where to now?"

Click-*bing*.

HOME

Oh.

"But what about you?" Tom said. He meant the porcupine.

"Oh, don't worry about me." He sounded almost civil for once. "I'll get where I'm going."

Click-*bing*.

LET'S STEP ON IT

WE'RE CUTTING IT CLOSE AS IT IS

When Kate read books about kids who got to go on magical journeys, she never really believed that they ever wanted to go home at the end. But now she realized how badly she was missing her parents and how much she needed to be somewhere safe and familiar and stationary for a while, even if it was a little dull. As they steamed past glaciers and snow-fields and crags, Kate felt proud and happy about everything they'd done. But on top of that feeling, weighing it down like a paper-weight, was a heavy, heavy sadness. For the animals she'd never see again. For the baby pangolin who had no safe place to be. For the cat and the heron and the polar bear and all the animals out there who were just trying to survive in a world that had lost its balance.

Tom sat next to her on the other side of the cab. His face was tired and blank, too. Uncle Herbert had been right: The world was more interesting than it looked, but it was so much harder and more complicated, too.

The sky was gray, and a light, thin snow fell and melted into droplets on the windows. The tracks wound through a deep pine forest. It was getting dark, and the snow was going blue in the twilight. Kate had always loved snow—it made her think about sledding,

and being cozy indoors, and hot chocolate, and days off from school. She ate dinner in the dining car by herself, reading a book, and went to bed in her lovely fold-down bunk with the window above it. She wondered if it was for the last time.

Lying there in the darkness, she thought about what the *Silver Arrow* must look like from above, the way a bird would see it: puffing along through the snowy nighttime wilderness, small and determined, its headlight splitting the darkness. Its whistle sounded, and where before it had sounded huge and

triumphant, now it sounded sad and a little lonely—the sound of something far from home that had come a long way and still had a long way to go.

The next day it was snowing harder, and the wind started to howl. It was a real blizzard. The *Silver Arrow* pounded through the storm, cutting through the wind, its cowcatcher sending snow fountaining off the track on both sides. Kate and Tom lit the woodstove in the library and wrapped themselves in blankets, and the porcupine sat in his armchair—which by this time was quilled beyond repair—and told them stories about his hair-raising standoffs with mountain lions and fishers, which were the only animals with the gumption to seriously take on a porcupine.

(A fisher was nothing like a fishing cat, the porcupine explained. Fishers were actually members of the weasel family, but much larger and more vicious than weasels. And they didn't even eat fish! Another brilliant piece of naming by the humans.)

Kate went up to the engine to check on the *Silver Arrow*. The sun was setting, and they were crossing a frozen lake. The tracks ran right across the ice.

THIS MAKES ME NERVOUS

"Me too." Kate peered out into the snowy twilight. "How thick is this ice?"

I DON'T KNOW

IT WAS A WARM WINTER. AND IT'S VERY LATE IN THE SEASON

"It had better be pretty thick."

WHAT ARE YOU IMPLYING ABOUT MY WEIGHT

SORRY

I MAKE JOKES WHEN I'M NERVOUS

Kate took their speed up as far as she dared. The sooner they got off this ice, the better. The wind made snaky sidewinders of snow that slid across the frozen lake.

Crunch! Suddenly the whole train lurched and slowed for a second—then kept going.

"What was that?!"

I THINK THE ICE IS CRACKING

Oh no.

"That isn't good."

She gave the train all the speed she could, but a minute later it lurched again, harder this time.

I THINK WE JUST LOST THE CABOOSE!

This ice wasn't going to hold them much longer. Kate sprinted back toward the library car. She met Tom and the porcupine in the corridor, coming the other way.

"The ice is cracking!" Kate said. "We're losing cars!"

"We know!" Tom said.

Crunch! This time the train ground to a complete halt and everybody fell down in a heap. Kate banged her elbow on the floor hard enough to bruise. They could feel the engine struggling and straining to get moving again. The weight of the long train was dragging it back and down.

"Come on!" Tom shouted.

They raced each other forward to the engine.

I'M STUCK!!!

"Come on!" Tom yelled. "Come on!"

"You have to try!" Kate said.

"You can do it!" said the porcupine. "Probably!"

There was a snap and a crash behind them, and with a grinding, groaning effort, the *Silver Arrow* surged forward again. Kate looked back: Maybe it was the snow and the darkness but all she could see behind them was the tender and the passenger cars.

Were all the rest gone? The library? Her beloved sleeper car? The candy car? There were so many candies she hadn't tried yet! There was a whole jar of something called Ultimate Malted Milk Balls, which were like regular malted milk balls but coated in all three kinds of chocolate—milk, dark, and white. Now she'd never get to try them!

They'd been in some close scrapes before, but it suddenly occurred to her—as it had that very first night, when they'd plunged down the hill behind the house—that maybe this wasn't going to turn out all right in the end. They'd come so far, but maybe they weren't going to make it all the way. Maybe that was how this story ended.

Then there was a crack like almighty thunder, and the ice gave way right under them.

The *Silver Arrow* crashed down through it into the freezing black water. A massive geyser of steam exploded up all around the boiler.

"No!" Kate shouted.

"No!" shouted Tom.

"No!" shouted the porcupine.

Click-*bing*.

BLAZE!

The Roundhouse

THE *SILVER ARROW* WEIGHED 102.36 TONS. IT DID not float. It sank—fast. Lake water boiled all around it from the heat of the engine.

As panicked as they were, Kate and Tom had the presence of mind to slam the windows shut as fast as they could and close the door at the back of the cab. *That should delay our deaths by both freezing and drowning for a good two minutes*, Kate thought.

"Can you swim?" she said.

"Yes," said Tom.

"I know you can, I meant the porcupine!"

"I certainly can," the porcupine said proudly. "My quills are hollow, so they double as natural flotation devices!"

"Okay. Good to know."

I CAN'T SWIM

IN CASE YOU WERE WONDERING

"No, I figured."

Kate stared at the dark water climbing up over the windows. There was a sickening sinking sensation as the snowy evening disappeared overhead and the train slid down into the black lake. How deep was it? There was some length of time people could survive in freezing cold water, and Kate couldn't remember exactly what it was, but she knew it wasn't very long. Even if they did get out, they'd be soaking wet in the middle of a frozen lake, probably miles from anywhere. They would freeze to death for sure.

Maybe better to drown and get it over with. Thin jets of water sprayed in around the doors— the *Silver Arrow* wasn't made to be watertight.

"Tom," Kate said, "is this one of those times when you secretly know what to do even though I don't?"

"No!"

They were completely underwater now. She thought of the time they'd plunged into the ocean surf and down into the emerald tunnel of water, and how glorious and wonderful it was. This wasn't like that. This was dark and cold and doomed.

If they did die, at least Kate knew it was for a good cause. They'd done what they set out to do, and it mattered. She only wished it hadn't cost them so much.

The water pouring into the cab was so cold that her feet went numb as soon as it touched them. Kate shivered with her whole body. There was no sound as the engine touched bottom and settled on the floor of the lake. The water outside was pitch black. She wondered how far down they were. She wished— how she wished—that she'd just stayed a tree in the misty forest forever.

For a second she actually wondered if

maybe the steam engine could run underwater. Maybe they could steam along the bottom of the lake and up onto land again. But it was too cold, you couldn't build up enough steam pressure. And there were no tracks. She realized she would never see her parents again, and hot tears ran down her face. Kate took Tom's hand with one hand and the porcupine's spiny paw with the other.

"Tom." She was so cold and scared she could barely catch her breath. "I really am glad you came with me. Except for this part, obviously. In a s-s-second I'm going to open the d-d-door." Her teeth were chattering. Tom's face was pale, and his lips were blue. "We're all going to t-take a deep breath and t-t-try to swim out. Swim s-straight up—we'll want to climb out through the h-h-hole the train made in the ice."

Probably she should've said something more, but she was so cold and wet and terrified, it was all she could think about. Except for one more thing.

"Goodbye, *Silver Arrow*. I love you."

Click-*bing*.

GOODBYE

I LOVE

But at that moment the rising water in the cab reached the level of the firebox, and the fire hissed and went out.

The lights went out, too, and in the bitter-cold darkness more tears flooded Kate's eyes, not for herself but for the thought of the *Silver Arrow* spending the rest of its days here at the bottom of a cold, dark lake in the middle of nowhere, with only cold, silent fish to keep it company. That was one of the first things Uncle Herbert said: Never let the fire go out. It was what the *Silver Arrow* had been most afraid of. And now the firebox was as dead and dark as when she'd first seen it. She wondered what it felt like, cold water flooding into your brain and putting out your thoughts. Did it fall asleep and dream? Or was it just—nothing?

Shivering uncontrollably, Kate forced her numb fingers to grip the door handle and braced herself for what she was about to do.

But before she could open the door, the train dropped and settled even farther. It was sinking into the mud! Only now did Kate's mind go completely blank with panic. If there was anything worse than being frozen and drowned, it was being smothered in freezing mud, too. Buried alive. She scrabbled furiously at the window, but she couldn't feel her fingers anymore—

Then a very weird thing happened: They fell.

She felt the train break through the mud and drop through air, and for a second Kate was weightless, and her stomach flipped. Then, with a crash like a thousand pianos being dropped from a million-story building, the *Silver Arrow* landed on something solid.

Nobody moved. Gradually Kate became aware that water wasn't coming in anymore. In fact it was draining out.

"W-what is this?" Tom said. "What h-h-happened?"

"N-no idea."

Cautiously, very cautiously, she wondered if it was possible that they weren't going to die. She slowly opened the window and looked outside.

They weren't underwater or buried in mud. They were in an enormous underground room. It was completely round and lit by orange light from a giant roaring fireplace. The air was warm.

"Heat!" Tom pushed past Kate and out of the cab.

A silver fish from the lake was still flopping around on the floor of the cab. The porcupine looked at it thoughtfully, and then he ate it.

Animals, Kate thought.

Outside a man was standing with his back to the fire, watching them. His face was in shadow, but Kate had a pretty good idea who he was.

"Come on," Uncle Herbert said. "Come get warm. You must be freezing."

Tom was already by the fire, and Uncle Herbert bundled a blanket around his shoulders.

Kate climbed down and took a blanket, too. Then she climbed back up, wrapped the blanket around the shivering porcupine, and carried him down to get warm. Only then did Kate accept a blanket for herself and take her place by the fire.

She could feel that they were deep underground.

"I know that was a terrible scare," Uncle Herbert said. "And I'm sorry. But you've done well, Kate. I'm proud of you."

She stared dully into the fire, still shaking. She wasn't proud of herself. She was just relieved and tired and sorry.

"I lost the train," she said. "All the cars. Everything. And I let the fire go out."

"You did your job. Your job wasn't to bring the train home, it was to try your hardest and never give up, and you did it. That's all that matters."

"Adults always say that."

"Every once in a while we say something that's true. We say a lot of things that aren't, so it's hard to tell which are which, but that one is true. It is literally all that matters. There are always more train cars. It's a lot harder to find good conductors."

"But the fire went out." She felt hot tears of shame on her face again. "I wasn't supposed to let it go out!"

"It's going to be all right, Kate. Look."

He turned her around to look at the *Silver Arrow*. A crowd of workers had appeared from somewhere, and they were climbing all over it. They were spraying off the mud and muck with hoses and wiping its windows and its brass bell and its great black boiler with cloths and sponges and towels. There was even a pit underneath the train where workers were cleaning its undercarriage.

"Will it be okay?"

"It'll be good as new."

She supposed she would take his word for it.

"Where are we?"

"This is the Roundhouse." He gestured grandly at the circular room. "This is where trains come to get fixed up when something goes wrong."

She saw now that the fireplace wasn't just a fireplace, it was actually a huge forge, like a blacksmith would have.

"We're going to take care of you, too." He put one arm around Kate and the other around Tom. "If you go through there"—he indicated a door with his chin—"there's a hot shower and fresh clothes and something to eat. Off you go. We'll talk when you're feeling better."

The Beginning

IN A KIND OF PRIVATE UNDERGROUND LOCKER room, Kate took the longest and hottest shower of her life. She steamed herself for what felt like hours, till the last frozen cell in her body was thawed out and pink and she was completely warm to the core again. Then she dried herself off and got dressed.

She didn't even know what time it was anymore, but somebody had laid out a big breakfast of pancakes and French toast with maple syrup and melted butter on the side, and it was the most comforting thing she could imagine. She ate till she was stuffed.

Then she took another hot shower just to make sure she was all the way warm. Plus she was pretty sticky from all that syrup.

When she and Tom came back into the Roundhouse, the workers were just polishing the last of the *Silver Arrow*'s brass fittings and changing the huge bulb in its big front headlight. The train looked as good as new. They'd even restocked the tender with coal and water.

"Do you want to do the honors?" Uncle Herbert said.

He offered her a fancy foot-long wooden match. Kate knew what he meant.

The makings of a great big bonfire had been laid in the *Silver Arrow*'s firebox: loose paper, then dry sticks for kindling, then thick branches on top of that. Kate lit the match and touched it to the corner of a crumpled newspaper and watched the flames lick and spread. When the fire was good and steady, she and Tom shoveled coal from the tender on top of the wood. She watched the steam pressure rise in the pressure gauge.

It all felt comfortingly familiar; she'd done it so many times. But she was still waiting for something. . . .

Click-*bing*.

HI

Kate smiled through her tears.

"Hi."

There was not really any part of the *Silver Arrow* that she could hug, but she wished she could.

I'M BACK

"Are you okay?"

I FEEL GOOD

"I'm glad."

WAIT

WHAT JUST HAPPENED?!

She explained about Uncle Herbert and the Roundhouse as well as she could, but the whole time she was thinking, *It's really back. It's really all right.* Kate felt like she'd come back to life, too. She felt fresh and strong and restored.

When the train was all steamed up and white wisps of vapor were floating out of its smokestacks and pistons, the door to the cab opened and Uncle Herbert climbed in. He looked around, and his face had a melancholy expression for a moment. Like he was remembering something.

He turned to Kate and Tom.

"I wonder," he said, "if you could give me a ride to my car."

With a great rumbling, the whole train started turning in place. Looking out Kate saw that it was resting on an enormous turntable, almost like a record player, that could spin and point the train in whatever direction it needed to go.

When the turntable stopped, the *Silver Arrow* was pointed at the arched entrance to a dark tunnel.

Tom switched on the headlight and released

the brakes. Kate put the reverser all the way forward and slowly opened up the throttle. She couldn't help showing off a little. The train started to move.

"Do you mind if I—?" Uncle Herbert said shyly.

He reached one hand up toward the ceiling. "Go for it."

With a grin, Uncle Herbert pulled the handle and blew the whistle.

FOOOOOOOOOOOOOOOOOOOM!!!!!

They steamed down the dark tunnel for a few minutes—then they rolled unexpectedly out into an enormous train station full of soft gray diffuse light, with a lofty ceiling of glass and wrought iron. A big clickety sign showed the names of many distant places.

They passed another train, waiting at a platform—not a full train, just an engine and a tender. A boy a little older than Kate sat in the cab, and when he saw her he waved shyly and rang his bell.

Kate did the same.

"So—we're not the only ones?" she asked Uncle Herbert.

"There are others. Not many, not yet. But you're not alone."

A minute later the train burst out into the open air, and they were running fast through a twilight landscape. Trees and cars and lighted houses streamed past. It was a long time since she'd seen them—she and Tom had spent a lot of time in some very remote places. Now they were coming back to civilization.

Tom took the controls and brought the

Silver Arrow chuffing and chugging up to full speed. Kate was feeling recovered enough to start thinking about everything that had happened to her and about what was coming next.

Apparently, Uncle Herbert was thinking about the same things.

"You've had to do some hard things on this trip," he said. "Both of you. You worked hard. You learned new things. You made mistakes and you owned up to them. You were uncomfortable and disappointed and discouraged and scared, but you never felt sorry for yourself and you never gave up. Those are some of the hardest things a person can ever do."

"I guess." Kate felt embarrassed at all the praise. "I mean, they're not harder than, I don't know, winning a marathon or writing a symphony or whatever."

"But that's *how* people get to do all that stuff, Kate. Anybody who's ever done something really important got there by doing the things you've learned to do. And if you just keep doing them, you'll accomplish amazing things too. Things you never would've dreamed you could do."

"Hey, how do you know all this?" Tom said. "Mom says you're the laziest man she's ever met."

"That doesn't mean I don't know what I'm talking about," Uncle Herbert said, and that melancholy look crossed his face again. "Just more the theory than the practice. I was a conductor once, too. I just wasn't a very good one."

He took off his hat and showed it to them. In little letters stitched on the brim it said *The Twilight Star*.

"So that was your train," Kate said softly. "We found it. It's still there."

Uncle Herbert nodded.

"Your mother and I were both conductors, a long time ago. But we weren't like you, we couldn't keep going. When things got tough, we gave up." Uncle Herbert looked down at his feet. "She doesn't really remember—it's like a dream to her. But I think that's why she finds it hard to be around me. And you may have noticed she's not too fond of trains, either.

"I couldn't forget, though. I never stopped wanting to be a part of it. So now I help out with some of the magic. But I leave the driving to the experts."

A half hour later they chugged back up the scary hill they'd swooped down so long ago and back through the old woods, and then Tom was slowing the *Silver Arrow* down in their own backyard. He stopped it on the exact same spot where they'd started, though now it was facing in the opposite direction.

There was something new in the backyard: a lighted railway clock on a lamppost, like the ones they'd seen at so many of the stations they'd passed.

"Now listen," Uncle Herbert said. "The way this works, only a few minutes have gone by since you left. If you guys can sneak back into the house without your mom and dad hearing, they'll never know any of this happened."

"Really?" Kate said. "But—that's very

weird. Wait, *did* it all happen? It already feels kind of like a dream."

"I promise you it happened. Here." Uncle Herbert handed her the case with Grace Hopper's glasses. Solemnly he gave Foxy Jones back to Tom. "It's the realest thing that ever happened to you."

Just to be doubly sure, Kate felt her elbow where she'd banged it right before they'd sunk through the ice. Yes: The bruise was still there.

They climbed down out of the cab. If what Uncle Herbert had said was true, then technically it was still her birthday, she thought. Not her worst birthday after all, but her best. And definitely the longest.

Kate knelt down next to the porcupine.

"I'm so sorry," she said. "We never took you anywhere. Where do you need to go?"

The porcupine looked around critically.

"I suppose here is fine. Those woods we passed look promising. I'm not picky, you know."

"You absolutely are picky," Kate said.

"You're one of the pickiest creatures I've ever met!"

The porcupine thought about that. "Yes, I suppose I am. I'm definitely picky about my friends."

He promised to visit soon, then ambled off into the night.

"I just can't believe it's all over," Kate said.

Uncle Herbert gave her a funny look. "What do you mean, all over?"

"You know—the trip. The adventure. It's all finished."

"Kate, the adventure's never over! Listen to me." He put his hands on her shoulders and looked her right in the eyes. "Even when you're home, even when you're standing still, going nowhere, you're still traveling in time. For every second that goes by you're traveling one second into the future. Every second of every day you're going somewhere you've never been before. The adventure *never* ends!"

Kate thought she understood. "Thanks, Uncle Herbert. I feel a little better."

"Good." He straightened up. "But also the adventure is literally not over. You're leaving on the *Silver Arrow* again in three weeks."

"We—we are?"

"Now that you've completed your first journey," Uncle Herbert said, "you are both formally officers of the Great Secret Intercontinental Railway."

He took two thick, very official-looking pieces of paper out of the inside pocket of his banana-yellow blazer and handed one to Kate and one to Tom. They were covered in important-looking stamps and seals and signatures.

"These are your letters of commission. And here are your pins."

He pinned a little silver train onto each of their chests.

"And here's your schedule." More papers. "You're going to be busy. As I said, the world needs good conductors, now more than ever, and there aren't many of you."

His yellow Tesla was waiting in the driveway. He shook their hands solemnly, climbed in, and rolled down the window.

"Get some rest," he called. "Tom's birthday is coming up, and I'm thinking of getting him a submarine."

His taillights blazed red in the twilight as he drove away.

When he was gone Kate and Tom crept inside their warm, quiet house, full of all the old familiar sounds and smells. Kate slipped back into her own room. All her old stuff was still there, just the way she'd left it. Adventures were a good thing, a great thing, but it turned out that coming home wasn't all bad either.

Standing in the middle of her room, she took a deep, shaky breath. She could barely think with all the excitement that was blooming inside her. There was so much good that needed doing in the world, and she was going to do every bit of it that she could. She knew it wouldn't be easy, or simple, but she couldn't wait to get started.

She was just changing out of her conductor's uniform and into regular clothes when she heard footsteps in the hall.

It was her mother. Probably she was coming to tell Kate to stop sulking, which was fair, and that it was time for her birthday dinner. Kate snuck a look out the window at the great dark shape of the *Silver Arrow* in the moonlight, patiently waiting to take her somewhere new and amazing.

It was like the heron said: The old balance was gone—but it wasn't too late to find a new one.

About the Author

LEV GROSSMAN is the author of five novels, including the #1 *New York Times* bestselling Magicians Trilogy, which has been published in thirty countries and adapted for television. Grossman is also an award-winning journalist who spent fifteen years as the book critic and lead technology writer at *Time* magazine. He lives in New York City with his wife and three children.